POPULAR PUBLICATIONS  FACSIMILE EDITIONS

Detective Dime Novels #1
(April 1940)

Step into the thrilling world of 1940s comic book superheroes with the debut issue of *Detective Dime Novels!* Join the daring adventures of Doctor Thaddeus C. Harker, a scientific criminologist armed with wit and Texas charm. As he travels the country, solving mysteries and peddling his Chickasha Remedies, danger lurks around every corner. But that's not all—immerse yourself in the gripping tales of Nick Ransom, penned by the masterful Robert Leslie Bellem. Action, intrigue, and a dash of old-fashioned charm await within the pages of this pulse-pounding premiere issue.

Authors:

Edwin Truett, Robert Leslie Bellem, Murray W. Mosser, L.K. Frank, C.S. Montanye

Illustrators:

Emmett Watson, Stewet Campbell

Why Trained Accountants Command High Salaries

[—and how ambitious men are qualifying by the La Salle Problem Method]

GET this straight.

By "accountancy" we do not mean "bookkeeping." For accountancy begins where bookkeeping leaves off.

The skilled accountant takes the figures handed him by the bookkeeper, and *analyzes* and *interprets* them.

He knows how much the costs in the various departments should amount to, how they may be lowered.

He knows what profits should be expected from a given enterprise, how they may be increased.

He knows, in a given business, what per cent of one's working capital can safely be tied up in merchandise on hand, what per cent is safe and adequate for sales promotion. And these, by the way, are but two of *scores* of percentage-figures wherewith he points the way to successful operation.

He knows the intricacies of government taxation.

He knows how to *survey* the transactions of a business over a given period; how to show in cold, hard figures the progress it has made and where it is going. He knows how to *use* these findings as a basis for constructive policies.

In short, the trained accountant is the *controlling engineer* of business—one man business cannot do without.

Small wonder that he commands a salary two to ten times as great as that of the bookkeeper. Indeed, as an independent operator (head of his own accounting firm) he may earn as much as the president of the big and influential bank in his community, or the operating manager of a great railroad.

Some Examples

Small wonder that accountancy offers the trained man such fine opportunities—opportunities well illustrated by the success of thousands of LaSalle accountancy students.* For example—one man was a plumber, 32 years old, with only an eleventh grade education. He became auditor for a large bank with an income 325 per cent larger.

Another was a drug clerk at $30 a week. Now he heads his own very successful accounting firm with an income several times as large.

A woman bookkeeper—buried in details of a small job—is now auditor of an apartment hotel, and her salary mounted in proportion to her work.

A credit manager—earning $200 a month—moved up quickly to $3000, to $5000, and then to a highly profitable accounting business of his own which netted around $10,000 a year.

And What It Means to You

Why let the other fellow walk away with the better job, when right in your own home you may equip yourself for a splendid future in this profitable profession?

Business Control   Through Accountancy

Are you really *determined* to get ahead? If so, you can start at once to acquire—by the LaSalle Problem Method—a thorough understanding of Higher Accountancy, master its fundamental principles, become expert in the practical application of those principles—this without losing an hour from work or a dollar of pay.

Preliminary knowledge of bookkeeping is unnecessary. You will be given whatever training, instruction or review on the subject of bookkeeping you may personally need—and without any extra expense to you.

If you are dissatisfied with your present equipment—if you recognize the opportunities that lie ahead of you through home-study training — you will do well to send at once for full particulars. The coupon will bring them to you without any obligation, also details of LaSalle's convenient payment plan.

Check, sign and mail the coupon NOW.

In answering advertisements it is desirable that you mention DETECTIVE DIME NOVELS.

1

Detective DIME NOVELS

VOL. 1
No. 1

APRIL
1940

CONTENTS

Published bi-monthly by The Frank A. Munsey Company, 280 Broadway, New York, N. Y. William T. Dewart, President. Yearly, $0.50; single copies 10 cents; foreign and Canadian postage extra. Printed in U. S. A.

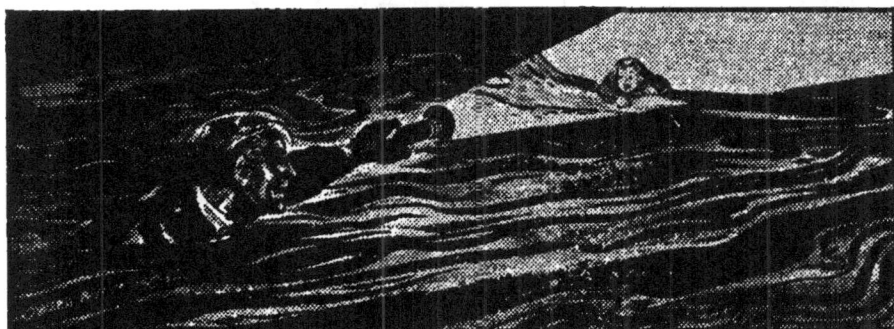

In answering advertisements it is desirable that you mention DETECTIVE DIME NOVELS.

3

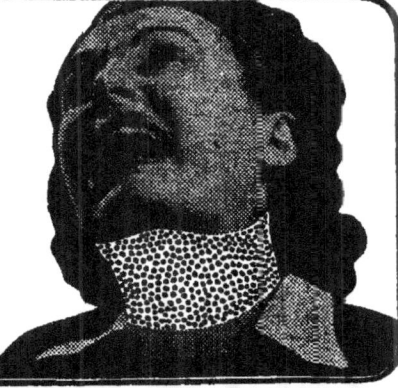

Crime Nest

By

Edwin Truett

"And suddenly, persons began to shoot at us from the underbrush"

Introducing Dr. Thaddeus Clay Harker who has his own peculiar remedy for rat-infested towns. A new Dime Novels' feature character

CHAPTER I

Meet Dr. Harker

*T*HE car itself was almost as gaudily painted as the peculiar t r a i l e r that swayed over the rain swept highway behind it. It was a twelve cylinder roadster, firewagon red, gleaming with chromium. All four sides of the red, box-like trailer were covered with enormous gold letters, proclaiming to any and all that Doctor Thaddeus C. Harker was bearing his world famous *Chickasha Remedies* to those in pain. Those signs went farther, to claim that *Chickasha Remedies* were a cure for practically every ailment of man and beast known to medical science, that no matter how greatly a man, woman or child suffered, he or

A Thrilling
Full-Length
Novel

she need not despair while the benevolent Harker and his world famous remedies travelled the highways and byways!

Hercules Jones drove the big coupe, a little sullenly, because he was lonesome. Herk Jones' liking for conversation and company was in just proportion to his size. He was six feet two inches in height, from the soles of his size twelve Oxfords to the top of his smoothly shaven pate. At one time Herk Jones, under various names, wrestled professionally and well among the country's foremost heavyweights. Doctor Thaddeus Clay Harker it had been who convinced him that the gathering of cauliflower ears and

7

bulging brows and flattened noses was hardly worth the game. Now, devoted to Harker, Herk Jones was a faithful adherent of *Chickasha Remedies,* as pitched from the rear end of the curious trailer.

The windshield wipers clicked rhythmically, keeping a pair of clean semicircles open to visibility in spite of the beating rain. The highway was practically deserted. Even the country looked barren and desolate, heavy with mesquite and yucca and tangled granjero, fit only for the raising of goats and sheep. Herk Jones flipped a button on the dash, saw a small light appear in the radio-like contrivance just left of the wheel, leaned toward the light.

"Well, well," came an impatient, drawling voice from the trailer, over the communication system, "are we at Abbottsville, are we even in Abbott County?"

Doctor Thaddeus Harker sighed the sigh of a man who has spent much time in the training of a recalcitrant child—and realizes that failure has been his only reward.

Herk answered defensively, "I just saw a sign, doc. We're about twenty six miles. You reckon Brenda is there and everything's okay?"

"Herk," he drawled, "you remind me greatly of the new hotel clerk who was so anxious to please."

Herk Jones beamed at the communicator. Maybe he had the doc started! Anything was better than sitting there looking at that white line unraveling so lonesomely down the water covered macadam!

"It seems," went on the doctor, "that a traveling man, arriving very late and worn out at this hotel, admonished the clerk that he wished to be awakened at six, as he had a train to catch. The clerk, in his efforts to be of unfailing service, went to the phone the next morning and called the traveling salesman. Sleepily the salesman somehow got to the offending instrument and growled his hello. 'This is the clerk,' said that worthy. 'Good morning, sir, you have a full hour yet to sleep.' "

Herk Jones' delighted guffaw filled the roadster. "Pretty good, doc," he bellowed. "Listen, did I tell you the one about the traveling salesman— It seems he—"

His face fell. He sighed disconsolately. The light in the speaking system was out. Evidently the little doctor knew the story. At least he turned off the speaker to keep from hearing it now. Hercules swept the car and the trailer over a concrete bridge, sighed again and sat back to finish the lonely drive into Abbottsville.

BACK in the trailer, Doctor Thaddues C. Harker wiped his glasses on a silk handkerchief, took a small pocket comb from a vest pocket and carefully combed his goatee and luxurious mustaches. He peered at his reflection in a steel mirror, took off the long chemist's smock and hung it on a hanger in a built-in cupboard. With the ease of a sailor on shipboard he walked the length of the swaying trailer. Near the rear, he reached behind a curtain, extracted a black hat with a wide brim, adjusted it carefully, donned a Prince Albert coat, reaching well toward the knees of his striped trousers and surveyed his reflection in another steel mirror, full length, which formed the rear and only door.

It was a peculiarity of the doctor that he never emerged from seclusion to appear before an admiring public, unless in full regalia. He looked greatly like the average conception of a

Kentucky colonel. It was easy to picture him, perhaps in the cool of the evening, on a broad porch with white columns, with a frosted mint julep in his blue veined hand, while soft-footed, colored servants administered to his wants and those of his equally gracious guests.

Yet behind that bland, old-fashioned countenance, beneath that silver white hair, lurked an amazing mentality. If truth be known, the good Doctor Harker was a medicine man because he liked it. It afforded him a means of covering the country without exciting suspicion, and, at the same time—because he was a pitchman par excellence, and eminently successful financially—also gave him means to indulge his real hobby. Harker's life hobby was scientific criminology.

The trailer, for example. True, one small locker held those potions and extracts necessary to the quick and efficient manufacture of *Chickasha Remedies*. With that one exception, the windowless trailer was devoted exclusively to criminology. Foldaway benches and cases held test tubes, microscopes, cameras for microphotography, instruments used in ballistics, and a fine array of books ranging from anatomy through toxicology to watermarks.

The air-conditioned trailer was Doctor Harker's place of refuge. There were, it is true, disguised slots in the steel walls which a man inside might peer at the passing country. Or even at approaching enemies. On occasion, it could, indeed, be used as a veritable fortress.

Now the Doctor flipped on his intercommunication. Herk Jones' displeased, "Yes, doc, what is it now," came to his ears.

"If you like," said the doctor's soft voice, "I will ride with you the rest of the way to keep you company. I am well along with my work."

Almost immediately, or so it seemed, the trailer and the roadster pulled to a stop at the side of the road. Doctor Thaddeus Harker was standing in the door when his leather jacketed assistant opened it, an old-fashioned umbrella in his hand. This he extended to Herk, with the air of one conferring a favor, like an accolade. Doctor Harker was extremely fastidious about his personal appearance; he abhorred rain. So, safely sheltered from the elements, he took his place in the big red roadster, while Herk started the car and headed on toward Abbottsville.

The breast pocket gave forth a vile, black, twisted stogie. A lighter in the dash did the dirty work. Herk cautiously lowered the window on his side to allow the heavy blue smoke to drift out.

Presently, he said, plaintively, "Doc, you and me and Brenda have been together darn near three years." The doctor sighed, he knew what was coming. He had heard this complaint many, many times before. "The thing is," went on Herk, "that after three years you ought to trust the two of us a little more, so we could—well, now, maybe help you more."

"You and Brenda," said the little doctor, "have always done very well indeed in my behalf." The malodorous smoke poured from nostrils, from his thin lips.

Herk coughed, looked at him resentfully, "But here's what I mean, doc," he continued aggrievedly. "You take this here Abbottsville we're coming to, now."

"That," admitted Harker smiling like a cherub, "is exactly what I mean to do—to take Abbottsville."

Herk Jones snorted. "Now see? That's what I'm talking about! We don't ever drive no four hundred miles without making a pitch. Why Abbottsville? You got something up your sleeve. And you'd do a lot better if you told me and Brenda everything, understand, so if it came to a pinch we could use our head. We got sense, too."

The doctor sighed. Herky hurried on.

"Now put yourself in our place. Two months ago we were in St. Louis, and you solved the Norton kidnapping!"

He said it in a tone of voice that might have been an accusation that the doctor committed the kidnapping rather than solved it!

"You had me running around doing silly things. You had Brenda running around doing silly things. Oh, I'll admit they worked out all right, but the point I'm making is that neither of us knew you were working on the Norton snatch until you had everything lined up and the police had made the kill." He sighed.

So did the doctor. Gently Harker said, "But you remember, Hercules, I saw to it that you got a lot of the credit, didn't I? And a thousand dollars of the reward?"

"Brenda didn't get no credit!" Hercules Jones did more than merely admire Brenda Sloan, the third member of the entourage. He was as faithful to her as a dog.

"BRENDA loses her value," said Harker gently, "once it becomes known that she is an associate of ours. And has it ever occurred to you, Hercules, that occasionally we, you and I, run into physical danger?"

Herk snorted.

"I promised Tom Sloan, Brenda's father, years ago that I'd take care of his little girl, Hercules. Is that your idea of taking care of her—to let her run the same risks that we run? No, she can help immensely—through being apparently unconnected with us, by doing exactly as she is doing now—going ahead and laying the groundwork."

"For what, doc? That's what I'm getting at. Why are we going to this town of Abbottsville? I know you got a letter from an old friend of yours some weeks ago. I know you sent Brenda on to Abbottsville right after that. Then we hang around nearly a month before we start out! What do we do in Abbottsville? Nothing ever happens in a town that size! Even if it is a resort town."

"We sell *Chickasha Remedies*," said the doctor gently. And, at the look of disgust on Herk's face, "Really, I can't tell you right now, Hercules. You'll see Brenda again—which will make you feel much better. But in the meanwhile you'll— Great Godfrey!"

The ejaculation was occasioned by the passing of a car. Now Hercules Jones invariably held the red roadster and ornate trailer around fifty on the highway. But the car that passed them was speeding so fast they might well have been standing still. It careened over the hill some quarter mile ahead, leaving Hercules to curse behind him. Hardly had Hercules relaxed his startled grip on the wheel when—"Great Godfrey!" said the doctor again.

A second car shot past them, traveling as recklessly as the first. It, too, shot over the hill, and out of sight.

Excitedly the doctor said, "The first was a coupe, the second a sedan! Suppose, Hercules, you travel a little faster for the nonce?"

"Not me," said Hercules, "not me with this trailer hooked on! Them guys can flirt with death if they want to!

They ain't hauling fifteen or twenty thousand dollars' worth of instruments in the back! Let 'em go, doc. I ain't moving this load any faster than now."

Doctor Thaddeus Harker merely sighed. He knew nothing could move the big man once he had the safety of those instruments at heart!

So, keeping at the same speed they went on over the wet highway, the rain beating at the windshield, the wipers clicking rhythmically. Eventually, they caught up with the coupe. From the brow of the hill they saw it, in the hollow below, near a concrete culvert. Miraculously it sat upright, yet the soft tire marks due to the rain, plainly showed that it had swerved complete-ly off the highway, down into the ditch itself, then swept back again onto the shoulder! Not twenty feet from the upward leading tracks was the omni-potent culvert.

Open mouthed, Herk braked the red coupe and trailer. He leaped out into the rain and approached the car just as the driver emerged. The driver was man of perhaps thirty-five, of meduim height, with calm, light blue eyes set in a swarthy face. He wore a light col-ored snap-brim hat, a dark topcoat with the collar turned well up and a pair of violently yellow gloves.

He grinned, "Close one, that, wasn't it? Mister, I was lucky to be able to pull back on the highway! Fool for luck, I guess."

Doctor Thaddeus Harker had raised his big umbrella, had left the red car. Now he stood behind the dark coupe, gazing at the left rear wheel. The tire was flat, blown out. Pieces of tube lit-tered the highway and ditch.

The stranger shook his head rue-fully. "Well, that's the way it goes. Lucky a front tire didn't blow out, isn't it? I'd have never headed it!"

Doctor Harker said, drawling his disapproval, "You must have been hit-ting eighty, my friend, and anything can happen at that speed. My man, Mr. Jones, will be glad to help you change the tire."

The stranger smiled. There was something cold and traplike about the expression of his mouth that cancelled the meaning of the smile. He looked toward Abbottsville once, then shrugged slightly, thrust out his hand to Herk. "Glad to know you, Mr. Jones," he said. "My name is Stanley." Now the hand was extended toward the doctor. The snap-brimmed hat indicated the big trailer. "And you're Doctor Harker, I suppose?"

Doctor Thaddeus Harker admitted his identity, shook hands and went back to the warmth and security of the red coupe. He opened the glove compart-ment, extracted a pair of German opera glasses and began peering at the coupe ahead of him. The opera glasses seemed scarcely to move. But no detail of that coupe's appearance skipped the shrewd, blue eyes of the doctor.

There was a bit of trouble; as there always is in the rain. Neither jack would go beneath the rear axle of the car, due to the softness of the road shoulder. Doctor Thaddeus Harker grinned at the look of amazement that overspread Mr. Stanley's face at Her-cules Jones' action. Very calmly Her-cules backed to the wheel, leaned down, grasped it with two hamlike hands, and raised the rear end of the coupe enough that the jack could be properly inserted.

In a trifle less than ten minutes, Mr. Stanley, who drove cars eighty miles an hour on wet highways, donned his topcoat, shook hands with his bene-factors and headed on toward town. Once inside the car, Hercules chuckled.

"Nice guy," he said broadly, "but he drives too fast. Have a nice nap?"

Doctor Harker looked at him in mild disapproval. "A little while ago," he chided gently, "you were complaining because I take neither you, nor Brenda into my confidence. May I illustrate my reasons, Hercules?" Hercules wrinkled his great brows.

"What did I do now?"

"Not what you did, but what you didn't do! From all indications, that is, from what you gathered, please tell me what happened back there."

Hercules drove on slowly, his brow working. "Well," he said doubtfully, "there's a guy named Stanley that sells cosmetics, and he's on his way to Abbottsville hitting eighty in the rain. He has a blowout, left rear, skids off the pavement someway, runs right into the ditch and back again, and I help him change a tire."

Doctor Harker shook his head. "You've overlooked the sedan," he said gently. "The sedan evidently was in pursuit of the coupe. You overlooked the bullet hole through the fender, and the fact that the tire was evidently exploded by a bullet, or bullets. And one other little thing of no particular consequence, Herk. Cosmetic salesmen seldom carry guns, and our friend, Mr. Stanley, undoubtedly had a gun in a holster beneath his arm. Nor do Chevvy coupes ordinarily come equipped with bulletproof glass!"

Hercules Jones looked properly chagrined. "I was so busy helping the guy," he began and broke off.

Doctor Harker was saying, "I think, Hercules, that we'll find Abbottsville very interesting indeed, in spite of its smallness! Now, if my information is correct, the Resthaven Courts should be on the right, just before we pass the city limits."

CHAPTER II

Detailed Information

ONE of Doctor Harker's unfailing characteristics was his courtesy. Cronies acknowledged that, at times, his flow of profanity was nothing less than phenomenal, yet contended that the little doctor could cure a man, or a situation, in seven languages, and yet do it politely! But it was around women, particularly beautiful women, that the doctor's manners waxed and blossomed to their fullest beauty!

Consequently, when Hercules Jones swung wide the door of the Resthaven Courts office and held it for the doctor's entrance, Harker became the epitome of courtliness, for the woman behind the counter was a thing of beauty.

"Come right in," she beamed, eyes widening at the doctor's magnificent appearance, red lips parting to exhibit teeth unbelievably white. The indirect light gleamed on the precise waves of hair exactly the same color as a new copper penny. "Welcome to Resthaven!" Her voice had that husky, throaty timbre that went up and down a man's spine!

The doctor's hat swept from his silver locks, his heels clicked, and the hat fell into place over his heart as he bowed with old world grandeur from the waist. "Ma'am," came his softly modulated voice. "I can only assure you that the pleasure is, indeed, all ours! Believe me sincere when I say that coming out of that raging torrent outside into a haven such as this, doubly made restful by the presence of a beautiful woman, is—ah, I can only say the place is correctly named, truly a haven of rest for the weary!"

If the Venus of registration was overcome by the profuseness of Doctor Thaddeus Harker's greeting, it didn't show on her features. Rather she managed to blush prettily, to drop her eyes, to raise long, red-tipped, slim fingers to the delicate coils of her hair. By now, the doctor was at the counter. She said, "How many in your party, mister?" At the same time pushing registration cards across the counter toward the beaming doctor.

"Two," he answered, disregarding the cards momentarily and twirling the left bar of his mustache. "A double cabin, if you will be so kind, ma'am. I am Doctor Thaddeus C. Harker, and this is my assistant, Hercules Jones." Now his own blue-veined hands reached for the registration cards. Behind him, he sensed Hercules open-mouthed, struck dumb at this vision of feminine pulchritude.

She observed the Spencerian script flowing from the doctor's pen with obvious pleasure, "I'm Mrs. Wright," she said, still coyly, "and I feel sure number 34 will suit you fine and dandy. I—"

"Charmed, indeed, to know you, Mrs. Wright," beamed the doctor. "I, too, am positive *any* accommodation assigned to us humble ones by a lady such as yourself will prove more than satisfactory."

Herk Jones' awed approval was little by little changing to disapproval—and worry. The doctor was carrying the palaver a bit too far—even for the doctor. Hadn't he seen that opening door? Hadn't he seen the man who entered so unobtrusively, on catlike feet, who now leaned against the doorway cleaning his nails?

Herk nudged the doctor with his knee.

The man in the door wore a brown suit, with a tan shirt, a tan tie. His hair was wavy and blonde, his face ruddy and almost beardless, but Herk Jones had been around. He knew the types. The man in the door was dangerous, he might as well have had a "Handle With Care" sign printed across him! Maybe he was the dame's husband, and maybe he was jealous!

And lookit! The damn' doc, in taking the key from Mrs. Wright's hand, had taken her fingers in his, was bowing over them. Again Herk nudged Doctor Harker.

"I'm sure, my dear," Harker went on, "my man and I will enjoy every day of our stay with you and Mr. Wright!"

She of the penny-colored hair beamed. "I hope so, Doctor. But as for Mr. Wright—!" She sighed. Her full bosom rose and fell. "Mr. Wright has been dead two years!"

Doctor Thaddeus Harker might have broken into tears of commiseration, except that the brown man, who, finishing his nails and putting the file in his pocket, advanced.

Funny, thought Herk, fascinated, how this new guy talked. That was it, tough! His chin dropped, a narrow black slot appeared beneath his nose and words came out of it. "I'll help stow 'em away, Jeannie."

Mrs. Jeannie Wright smiled at him, introduced him as her brother, George Vasey, and extracted the key from the doctor's hand. Doctor Harker said, "Hercules, please go to 34 with Mr. Vasey, put the trailer and car in the correct spots, stow our luggage and return for me."

Herk Jones eyed George Vasey like one strange dog eyeing another. What was it about the man he disliked and mistrusted so greatly? Ordinary as to height and clothing, ordinary as to features, except for that slot of a mouth. And eyes! That was it, eyes! The guy didn't give you a chance to look at his eyes! He kept them fixed right on a guy's belt buckle when he talked. And Hercules had a curious thought then. The guy kept looking at a guy's middle like he was thinking how he'd enjoy sticking a knife there. And maybe twisting. He'd have to tell Doc Harker that, Hercules decided as he shook the umbrella, left it in a corner and went out the door.

For a moment George Vasey stood before the office in the rain staring at the red coupe and trailer. Inside the coupe Herk started the motor, glared at the sinister one. Vasey turned, shrugged his shoulders, started down the gravelled passageway toward number 34. Exclusive sort of guy, thought Hercules, his dislike rampant. From long experience at tourist camps Jones knew the customary thing for Vasey to have done would have been ride the running board and direct the incoming guest. Vasey didn't. He merely walked down the drive to the very last cottage, unlocked the door, flipped on the lights and stood in the lighted doorway, not even watching the masterful maneuvering of the trailer and coupe.

AFTER some five minutes Hercules Jones had both in place, one beneath each shelter of the double cottage. He opened the rear of the coupe, unloaded the luggage and brought it into the cottage, George Vasey merely drawing back enough to give him leeway. Finished, Hercules realized that although Vasey had seemingly been unaware of each movement, he actually had taken the opportunity to eye each piece of luggage. Arms akimbo, Hercules faced him, the short hair on the back of his neck actually bristling.

He said, "Okay. Well?"

Vasey's eyes sought and found Herk's belt buckle. He said, "You guys aim to stay long?"

Hercules said, "Why?"

The brown shoulders shrugged. "I wouldn't. You got guts bringing a nostrum into a town like Abbottsville. Health center, hot springs and mineral springs, three doctors to every block, and up pops a pitchman. You won't last long."

Hercules seethed. "Listen, chum, Doc Harker has got something the rest of these monkeys never will have. Pitchman, sure, but he's no fake. And you can bet six, two and even we'll stay as long as we like! We got a state license."

Vasey's jaw dropped. The slot appeared. Sounds like *Heh! heh!*—Three of them only. He said, "You don't know this bunch of medicos here, son, They'll have you in the jailhouse if you fool with them. You ought to be wise and skip it."

Hercules didn't deign to answer. He put his hand on the door-knob. Vasey shrugged, turned, went out into the rain. Hercules stood there watching him go suspiciously, until he headed left toward the lighted office. What was there about the guy that was a challenge? Just because he looked like a movie gangster?

Herk locked the front door, pulled the shades, went out the back door carefully and locked it, too, behind him. While the big man was given more to brawn than to brains, once he learned his duties, he could be depended upon to perform them as faithfully as a well trained dog. Many a time in the past he had done the very thing he was setting out to do right now. He knew that Doctor Thaddeus Harker didn't expect him back in the office at once. He knew he was to explore the tourist camp, to learn if possible all angles, all possible alleyways of escape in a hurry should such a thing be necessary. He was to get his key impressions, and a half dozen other things which he did not thoroughly understand, but which he was always obliged to do by his employer.

With the collar of his l e a t h e r jacket turned up he moved about the U shaped court amazingly quiet for so large a man. The cottage next door, number 32, was unoccupied.

From a pocket of the l e a t h e r jacket Herk t o o k a blank

> To whom it may concern:
>
> I can recommend Dr. Harker's Chickasha Remedies. He made a new woman of me.
>
> (signed) Brenda Sloan

key, covered with a soot-like substance. This he inserted in the lock, twisted each way, then dropped it into an envelope similar to those used by paymasters. With a stub of a pencil, there in the rain and darkness, he inscribed the cabin number.

All together, on the way back to the office, he made sixteen cabins, all that ranged that side. On those that were obviously vacant he took key impressions. Five were occupied. At the doors of two of these—all he dared risk at the moment—he knocked and made some inane request. A pair of pliers to be borrowed. A pair of pliers to be returned—the returner eventually finding he had made a mistake. But under each pretext he was enabled to view at least one occupant of the cabin.

Doctor Harker liked to know who his neighbors were, under all circumstances.

Eventually Hercules got back to the office, to find Doctor Thaddeus still industriously complimenting the Titian-haired Mrs. Wright. On Hercules' appearance, he bowed his adieu in courtly manner and went out into the elements beneath the enormous umbrella held by the hand of the retainer.

"Lookit, doc," said Hercules, "what is there about the dame's brother that upsets me so much? How come I can look at him and get a mad on?"

Doc l a u g h e d. "George, I believe, has s e e n too many gangster pictures." He sighed. "I never yet saw a beautiful woman t h a t didn't have a drawback of one kind or another. Jeannie's is evidently her brother."

Hercules opened the cabin door, the doctor led the way in. "As usual," said the doctor, "you missed the most important thing about George. He was dressed in dry clothing, dry shirt, dry coat and pants, but his feet were so wet he actually squished when he walked. Mmmmmm."

Hercules grinned. The doctor was always noticing things like that. And what difference did they make? He laid the envelopes on the dresser, told Harker in a few words about the occupants of the cabins. Very meticulously Thaddeus Harker wrote the information in a notebook. Finished with Hercules, he kept on writing, speaking aloud slowly and distinctly.

Thaddeus Herker was a past master at extracting information from one who was, as a rule, altogether unaware of what was going on. Now, as he spoke and inscribed for future reference the facts of Mrs. Jeannie Wright's life and career, Hercules grew more and more amazed. At last he said.

"Now just why in the hotel do you want to know that about a red-headed dame? Sometimes I think you're so used to asking questions that—oh, what's the use! I got to finish up. How about something to eat?"

Harker clicked the notebook closed, put it away, drew an enormous silver turnip of a watch from his pocket. He nodded, as if to say he agreed with the watch. "We shall dine, my boy," he said, smacking his lips at the thought, "like the gentlemen we are! Martinis, perhaps, and most certainly filet of anchovies, ripe olives and hearts of artichokes. A fine rare steak then, and perhaps—" he waved his hand—"perhaps we'll see Brenda. Now go about your work, my boy. I want to clean up a bit myself."

HERCULES JONES went out the back door once more. He circled the cottage on those huge, noiseless feet, to see if they were being spied upon. Why they should be, he didn't know. He only knew the doctor insisted on such precautions. He walked again to the head of the drive, peered surreptitiously through the window into the office. Mrs. Wright and her brother, George, were there. Mrs. Wright was doing a repair job on her complexion. Brother George was sitting. Just sitting and nothing more, his eyes peering down at his extended feet. His posture made Hercules remember what Thaddeus Harker had told him about the wet shoes. But now Brother George was wearing a pair of two-toned sports shoes, and because his heels were on the floor, and his toes pointed well upward, even Hercules Jones could not but note and comment on the dryness of those shoes. His inner comment, however, was simply a sarcastic observation that Brother

George, who saw too many gangster pictures, was a nut about changing his clothes. Particularly his shoes.

He passed behind the office and over to the other side of Resthaven. Seventeen cabins confronted him, and there he did exactly as he had done on the other wing of the U. Carefully he marked the envelopes containing his keys. Beaming and ingratiatingly, like a huge tail-wagging dog, he borrowed pliers and screw drivers from those cottages that were occupied, in order to see who stayed within. Whenever it was possible, he found out how long they had been there, as well as when they meant to leave. Whenever a car was parked beneath the adjoining shelter, he took the license number. Herk Jones was well trained. His not to reason why the Doctor wanted this detailed information! Oh no—all he had to do was to *get* it! And foolish or not, Herk got it!

Nearing the back of the grounds, he was surprised to see that the building there was not a barrack-like dwelling, as he thought. Rather it was a garage, for four cars, each of which, unlike the open shelters adjoining the cabins, bore a door. Two were locked. Two were unlocked. Those that were open were empty. He stood there in the rain swearing, thinking of the meal Harker had outlined, thinking of the possibility of seeing Brenda Sloan.

The pass keys on the ring in his pocket opened the first garage. He found there a black sedan, duly noted its license number, examined it with his small flashlight and locked the door the way he had found it. The second locked door was stubborn. He toiled in the rain, his brows knit, swearing because the lock could not be picked.

Herk Jones was not a professional strong man for nothing! He thrust a great forefinger through the hasp, the stubborn lock resting in the palm of his hand. He made a pad of his handkerchief, laid it over the lock and inserted forefinger. To a man who drove nails with his fist, what followed was not so hard. He simply balled his right fist, raised it perhaps twelve inches, and brought it down viciously on the handkerchief pad. Three times Hercules did this before the staple gave way and released the lock in his hand.

He grunted, thrust it into his pocket, meaning to put it back, entered the last garage. After this, he was thinking, something to eat—and Brenda! But the first gleam from his pocket flash drove such thoughts from his mind.

Due to Doctor Thaddeus Harker's persistent and painstaking training, Herk's memory, while not phenomenal was, at least, above average. *The license plate revealed by his flash was that of the coupe that had run off the road some fifteen miles from Abbottsville not two full hours ago!* The coupe, which, according to Doctor Harker—and Herk admitted to himself that the doctor was usually right—had suffered a blowout and rear wreckage because of a bullet! The coupe of the man named Stanley! Who carried a gun!

Wide eyed, open mouthed, he moved to the left side. There was the bullet hole! Where was Stanley, then? He hadn't been in any of the occupied cabins. Of course, he could be somewhere else, he might be checked into one of those cottages from which Herk had gotten a key impression. But—hell, here was his car, he *had* to be somewhere close!

He was close, all right. In the car. He was contorted beneath the wheel, shoved down onto the floor. His face was black, his eyes protruding, his tongue out. Both hands were still raised, toward his neck! And the neck itself! Long strips of skin had literally been clawed from the throat. Around it, ran a slight crease, as if two edges of loose skin had been pulled out and somehow brought together.

And it was only by cautiously opening the door and putting his own face inches from that of the dead man that Herk saw the wire garrotte buried in the blackened, nail-torn flesh of the neck. One end of the wire protruded some six inches, bent upward now beneath the left ear. By close examination, the strong man saw that the garrotte was a loop of piano wire threaded through a contrivance that allowed it to be pulled tight like a hangman's noose, and evidently preventing it, by grip or friction, from being loosened. The gadget, oval in shape, was approximately two inches in length, perhaps half an inch in width. It, too, was partially buried in blackened flesh.

This, Hercules knew, was something for Doctor Thaddeus Harker! Not for Hercules Jones to figure out the whys! It was enough for him to find a dead man! He felt a pang of pity for Stanley as he closed the car door. After all he'd seemed like a nice enough guy. And a sudden thought struck him—was the sedan in the other locked garage the one that had speeded past them in pursuit of the Stanley coupe?

He hurried from the garage, wrapped in the new thought, turned to close the door. Whoever and whatever hit him, he decided afterward, was both proficient and merciless. The first vicious blow would have killed an ordinary man. It merely spun Hercules about, but his senses were so addled, the lights dancing before his eyes were so multicolored and so glaring that he could make out nothing. The second blow felled him, and even as he went down he received a third blow that sent him to merciless blackness.

CHAPTER III

A Letter to Read

*H*ARDLY had the door closed behind Hercules Jones when Doctor Thaddeus Harker set about his ablutions. Doctor Harker was a fastidious man, to extremes. He hung the Prince Albert coat carefully on a hanger on the inside of the closet door; he extracted a paper sack from the over-sized portmanteau of indefinite years and fondly placed his hat inside of it before stowing it on the upper shelf of the same closet.

The removal of the white-piped vest, the black string tie and the soft, white, pleated shirt, disclosed long sleeved underwear, grey in color, light in weight. The portmanteau yielded an array of other things that was astonishing. There were felt house slippers; an old fashioned straight - bladed razor; a worn strap; a Swaty hone; monogrammed shaving mug; well - worn brush; shaving lotion; bay rum, of course; hair tonic, and a tremendous can of after-shaving talcum. With the exception of the slippers, all of these things were placed on the bureau. For Doctor Thaddeus C. Harker disdained and mistrusted modern bathroom conveniences. For nearly fifty years he had shaved before a dresser or bureau, and nothing else would suit him.

Later, a casual observer might have giggled a bit at his rare appearance as the well-worn blade of the freshly-stropped razor cunningly swept over the pink cheeks. For he wore his long underwear, his house shoes, and the wide belt around his rounded waist resembled, more than anything else, a corset.

Finishing, he rinsed his instruments in the granite pan, emptied the pan, laid the array of tonsorial articles in a neat and meticulous line at the back edge of the bureau. He whistled—perhaps he was thinking of the Widow Wright—while he sprinkled hair tonic liberally on his silver hair, rubbed it in, combed it and brushed it with a pair of military brushes until it gleamed and glistened. The moustaches and the goatee came in for their share of grooming.

Doctor Harker had one disappointment, however, that evening that threatened to spoil the whole thing. The bathroom was merely a shower! So Thaddeus Harker contented himself with a sponge bath, taken in the same pan he had used for shaving. Ten minutes after the bath, resplendent in newly-laundered linen, the vest in place and the coat and hat awaiting his pleasure, he glanced at his huge silver watch. Herk was late. But the doctor was philosophical. He even smiled a bit thinking Herk might be enjoying a little talk with Jeannie Wright—work done. And there was time, plenty of time. He lit a cigar.

Ten minutes passed slowly, all too slowly. During that time Doctor Harker extracted a bottle of bourbon from the voluminous portmanteau, and with much cautious lifting of the moustaches, downed two quick shots. As usual, the pleasant warmth in his stomach, rather than making him drowsy, aroused greater energy in his brain. *Chickasha Remedies* faded away. The walls of the tourist cottage dissolved; and all thoughts of Hercules Jones disappeared from his mind.

Thaddeus Harker was a young man

again, and, strange as it might seem, considering his present occupation, was a student in a pharmacy college! His bosom friend, the man who played Damon to his Pythias, was rotund, red-cheeked Arthur Wallace.

A faint smile overspread Doc Harker's features, as, with closed eyes, he contemplated his past. He recalled half-forgotten episodes, the fabric of youthful dreams, the dates together, promises to stick together, no matter what! Harker's thin shoulders shrugged. He opened his eyes. He poured another drink. For, as usual, these promises hadn't been kept—the pair of friends had drifted apart. Yet they had corresponded, from year to year. One Christmas, in Rio, Harker's lone touch with home had been Wallace's letter. Another had overtaken him in China; still another in Europe. And during all of this, Harker's, peregrinations, Wallace had played the part of local boy who stayed home and made good. For Wallace had purchased a part interest in a small pharmacy in this very town of Abbottsville.

Abbottsville itself was peculiarly situated physically. The countryside for miles around presented the typical mesas of the southwest, cactus covered, fit only for the raising of sheep or goats. Yet, for an area of perhaps two square miles, the town was surrounded by abrupt hills and cliffs, a volcanic rock formation tossed carelessly skyward by a mighty Mother Nature some millions of years before. The valley formed by these hills was sheltered from all winter wind and northers. Hot springs, trickling and gushing profusely from the rocks, seemed to heat the very ground, to keep unpleasant winter at a distance.

No one had thought much of these springs, except as natural curiosities, until Arthur Wallace, practising chemistry as a hobby, had analyzed some of the waters and found them profuse in body-building minerals and health-producing salts. He had found a way to crystalize these waters, to box the crystals and so to keep them indefinitely.

Wallace had always been, as Harker remembered him, a poor business man. Either that—or he was a humanitarian. For he shipped his Abbott Crystals far and wide at such cheap prices that practically any sufferer, no matter how poor, might buy them. It had been outside capital that came into the town and bought more of the springs, that built the two resort hotels, and advertised the town discreetly as a health resort.

Doc Harker sat there in the rocking chair and turned the word *discreetly* over in his mind. There was no doubt in the world, he reasoned, that with the proper exploitation, Abbottsville could have become another Hot Springs or French Lick. Why, then, had it held back? Why wasn't it better known to the American public, through advertising, radio, newspapers and magazines? Perhaps the letter in his belt held the answer.

HIS fingers opened his vest, his shirt, undid the catch on one of the compartments of the corset-like belt. He drew out the letter from his old friend Arthur Wallace, written more than four weeks before, that had brought him at this late date to the small, unimportant resort town of Abbottsville.

The first few paragraphs were ordinary, exactly what could be expected from one old friend to another, telling of families, business experiences, touching on past occasions of their youth. It continued:

"—so Thaddeus, strange things have trickled back to my ears, at times, concerning some of your activities; things which have appeared to me to be more in line with your keenness and your abilites as I remember them than merely peddling patent nostrums about the country from a circus van.. You are a sly one, Thaddeus. Certain young men, who have worked for the government at times; certain young men, who have been connected with various law enforcement agencies, have told me tales of your ability in criminology. So, considering this, Thaddeus, I have a favor to ask of you.

"Having spent so many of your years roving, Thad, you can hardly appreciate the love a man may come to bear for a town. Mine for this town of Abbottsville, for example. I won't go into lengthy detail concerning how my grandfather helped to found it, how he passed his affection for it to my father, from whom I, in turn, inherited it. You remember our plans, yours and mine, when we were at school? How the world was to be our oyster? Suffice to say my love for Abbottsville was sufficient to overcome those roseate dreams—you went on, I returned. And Thaddeus, year by year, my love for the town has grown.

"Have you ever loved a beautiful woman with all your heart and soul, and watched her disintegrate from day to day? Watched her acquire habits— dope, drink, vice—which presently obtain such a hold on her that it is almost impossible for her to throw them off? On the surface the effects of these habits do not show. They are covered cunningly with make-up, rouge and mascara and powder. But to the man who loves her they are all too apparent. He knows that she is merely a shell of her former self.

"That has happened here in Abbottsville, Thaddeus. We have two expensive hotels and numberless smaller houses. Here, you may believe it or not, criminals seem to be immune to capture, national criminals. Wanted men and women walk our streets, and honest citizens—what few there are left—dare not report them to federal authorities. I say *what few there are left* because this element enriches our town, they pay huge prices for everything, and the ordinary citizen holds his pocketbook higher than his civic pride.

"There may be a few honest police officials, but I doubt it. Here is an example: What would you say if I told you part of the Courtland ransom money circulated almost openly here? I myself had some of it, several bills, and knew what it was. To my great shame, I was *afraid* to turn it over to the Federals. I simply got it out of my hands as quickly as possible.

"That is only one example. I think Abbottsville is one enormous sink of intercourse for criminal and semi-criminal, a meeting place! Loot is brought here, exchanged, distributed. Gamblers operate openly, as do brothels. I love this town, Thaddeus, I want it cleaned up. You have had success in the past at such things, can't you help me now? I needn't point out that I wouldn't blame you for passing us by—there is much danger involved. My son-in-law has been working quietly and beneath the surface for weeks collecting evidence that would incriminate some of our leading citizens. But I am afraid he is not the man for the work, since he is too well known.

"Three of us old timers have made up a purse to the man who cleans the town, Thaddeus. That purse amounts to $25,000. Now I must give you a few details, in case you expect to go into the thing.

"John N. Chambers, owner and operator of the two largest hotels, is the mayor. Chambers' only fault, to my mind, is his obvious lack of civic consciousness. I mean his complacency with Abbottsville as it is. I understand he was formerly a citizen of New York City.

"Carson Thames, head of the Police Department. Thames also is an outsider, having come here some eight years ago, a native of California. His fault, to my mind, is his blindness, assumed, or real."

Doctor Thaddeus C. Harker laid the letter aside. Again he dove into his corset-like money belt, came out with picture torn from a newspaper, the *Abbottsville Courier*. It was a group picture of a dozen men, officials and prominent citizens of Abbottsville, attending a banquet. This the doctor had clipped from the *Courier* on receipt of Wallace's letter. Every face was turned proudly and openly toward the camera. Several of these were ringed. And safe in Harker's trailer were the resulting blowups—or enlarged pictures—taken from the group shot. He examined it for a moment, then laid it on the table.

"Chambers, Thames, Melton, Carter, Maroni," he murmured aloud.

The letter continued, naming Melton as proprietor of The Southern Club, a gambling spot, and several questionable roadhouses in the adjoining hills. Carter was publisher of the *Courier*. Maroni was simply a local labor czar and a big man in Abbottsville politics.

"Here is the startling part, Thaddeus," the letter went on. "You know that on the first or second of November, Ray Zachary is to be released from

Atlanta. You know what that means. He will attempt to take over some of the racketeering, nationally, that he held before the income tax people put him away. Other racketeers will endeavor to prevent it. And I have it on good authority that Zachary has made arrangements to come to Abbottsville, to operate with my home town as his headquarters! Needless to say it will ruin Abbottsville."

CHAPTER IV

The Missing Picture

DOCTOR HARKER'S methods of working on such a problem were extremely unorthodox. In a way, he was a firm believer in the old adage concerning giving a man enough rope. His first move had been to send Brenda Sloan into Abbottsville to establish residence. Brenda was a past mistress at playing necessary roles. He provided her with money, but not too much money. She could speak wisely and knowingly and yet reveal nothing. Other than sending Brenda to the scene, Harker had not answered Wallace's letter.

The only word he had heard from the girl was the names and all information she could possibly contrive to obtain concerning the big men of Abbottsville. Harker, in turn, had taken this information and pried into the pasts of these men, painstakingly assembling every point, every detail of their past lives. This, true enough, had taken time, but in that trailer, cunningly hidden, was a complete dossier of all of Abbottsville's important men!

And one thing was outstanding! Although most of these men claimed various sections of the country as their o.iginal homes, each, the doctor found, came from one small section of the east, either from New York itself or nearby in Jersey! Vultures gathering, one by one! Jackals called to the feast by fellow jackals!

Carefully the doctor put the letter back into the wide belt. He looked longingly at the bourbon bottle, decided another drink might spoi¹ his appetite, dragged the enormous watch from his pocket and frowned portentously! That Hercules! He'd have to be spoken to for being so late, so long!

Tappety-tap-tap at the door. Doctor Harker called, "Who is it?"

"Only little me," cooed a voice in response.

The Doctor leaped into action. His Prince Albert came down off its hanger, his arms went into the sleeves. On the way to the door he shot his cuffs, adjusted his string tie. He opened the door and bowed courteously to the Widow Wright. "Welcome, welcome, ma'am," he beamed. "Won't you accept my poor hospitality, my shelter from the elements?"

She stepped in, smiling redly. She was wearing a colorless, oiled-silk, rain cape with an attached hood. Through that hood gleamed the copper colored hair, the dark clinging sweater and the short skirt that accented the curved lines of her figure. And safely sheltered from the rain her left arm was crossed with towels.

She threw back the transparent cape said, "Georgie couldn't remember whether there were clean towels or not, and I do so want you to be happy and satisfied while you're with us!"

She bustled about hanging the towels in their proper places. And finishing, she turned, noted the doctor's admiring eyes on her and flushed.

Harker said, sighing, "The woman's touch! Ma'am I can't tell you what it means to an old bachelor who has never known connubial bliss!" For a moment he looked as if he was about to break into tears. She actually extended a pitying hand. But he held his emotions, though a tear might well have gleamed in his eye.

"May I offer you a little refreshment, ma'am in return for your care and worry?"

He could—and did. The Widow Wright sipped her bourbon with apparent relish, and they spoke of those inconsequential things eternally spoken of between an elderly, though admiring, man and a beautiful young woman.

Another rap at the door. The doctor smiled. "Hercules Jones," he said, and sat his glass down. But when he opened the door, it wasn't Hercules, it was Georgie Vasey, the widow's brother. He stared at the exact center of the Doctor's round little stomach, said, "Mister, that big guy that drove you in has had an accident. He's back here by the garage, out like a light. Want I should help you bring him in?"

Doctor Thaddeus Harker reached for his umbrella. He even forgot his courtesy in his sudden flash of worry for the big man of all work. He failed to tell Jeannie Wright goodbye.

HERCULES JONES groaned and tried to open his eyes. This was extremely difficult, for someone was rubbing them with a wet towel. He was conscious of an arm beneath his head—a head that raged like a cauldron of blazing pain—conscious of a bottle against his thick lips. He parted those lips and almost strangled on the whiskey that was poured into his mouth. Gradually a wave of warmth swept upward from his stomach, his head began to clear a bit, the towel was jerked away and a kaleidoscope of faces spun before his unfocussed eyes. Hurriedly he closed them again.

He heard a man's voice saying, "— that's the guy okey, on account of he borrowed a pair of pliers from me not more'n an hour ago and somebody must have conked him and rolled him out—"

Then Doctor Harker's voice broke in. "Ridiculous! No one conked him, as you say. It is perfectly obvious he simply slipped and fell, that he butted his head against the steel post of this garage."

More liquor. Again the doctor's voice, "Hercules, Hercules, how do you feel?"

Eyes opened. The doctor's face swam into view, threefold. Someone was holding an electric lantern. As the features he knew so well dissolved into one moustache of great proportions and a solitary goatee, Herk was aware that over and over the doctor's left eye was winking, that the hand beneath him was squeezing in unison with the wink.

He sat up. Doctor Harker purred, "Herk, you clumsy oaf, how'd you happen to fall?"

"Just—just—slipped in—puddle—" managed Herk, catching on. He lumbered to his feet, shook his head like a great bull to clear his vision. Georgie Vasey held the lantern. He stood there looking—right at Herk's belt buckle.

The doctor said, "I certainly thank all you good people for your interest and concern. I think if I get him into the cottage now he'll be quite all right!"

With his arm about the doctor's shoulder, Hercules headed away—not toward—the cottage, but, as if dazed, back across the front of the garage. In a moment the doctor turned him. Hercules had seen enough to expel any lingering nausea. *Both the garages that had been locked were now standing wide open! Both the sedan and the coupe that had contained the dead man were gone!*

* * *

Jeannie Wright stood in the lighted door of their own cabin awaiting their coming. She cooed and made a fuss over Hercules; she insisted on a hot towel for his head; she made him take a drink he did not want. All the time he was seething with information, impatient for the woman to go. And at last she departed.

"Listen, doc," began Herk, excitedly, but Doctor Harker held up his hand.

"Just a minute, Hercules. You're too excited now. Into the bathroom for a hot bath, then you can tell me about it." And he pushed the giant into the bathroom, and a moment later heard the hiss of the shower.

Doctor Harker spent the ensuing few moments in kicking himself mentally. For the picture clipped from the *Abbottsville Courier* was missing from the table where he had laid it. No man could dabble in crime and criminology as long and as successfully as Harker without becoming suspicious of every circumstance.

No sooner had he entered the cottage, helping Hercules, than the thought had occurred to him—like a kick in the seat of the pants—that he had broken one of his self-made commandments. That commandment was to never be hurried into anything. Herk's accident and his sudden surge of fear—because of liking for the big man— had left the cottage untenanted for all of ten minutes. Untenanted?

The Widow Wright had been left there. And the marked picture from the newspaper was now missing. Two and two makes four. Now, the next thing, according to Harker's way of thinking was: Why should he take the apparently innocent picture? True, it was ringed. But, if she was an innocent widow operating a tourist camp, why wouldn't she merely look at the picture and leave it where it lay? He opened the portmanteau. Only an eye trained to detail, such as Harker's would have perceived that someone had gone through it!

Again he considered all angles. Someone. The widow? Maybe she *had* come out, maybe someone else had gone through the cottage. But there was one thing he *could* do. He drew a linen handkerchief from his pocket, wrapped it around the glass from which Jeannie Wright had taken her bourbon, and put it in one corner of the portmanteau. That, he thought, would do temporarily. It had been searched once and probably wouldn't be again for some time, at least not until he had time to stow it away in the steel trailer that was like a safe on wheels.

Hercules Jones, clad in fresh shorts only, came out of the bath. Water still gleamed on his shaved head, he glared at the doctor.

"Somebody did too conk me," he said belligerently, "and I got me an idea it was that monkey Georgie. Who found me?"

The doctor smiled. "Georgie, I believe. What did you chance upon that Georgie—if it was he—resented?"

"A dead man," said Hercules Jones grimly. "A stiff. The guy Stanley, the cosmetic salesman, with a wire gadget around his neck that choked him to death."

The doctor was on his feet excitedly now. His little blue eyes blazed, his moustaches quivered. "Where is the body?"

Hercules Jones picked up the bourbon bottle and drank noisily from the neck. He wiped his mouth on a hairy wrist, shook his sore head sorrowfully, said, "I wish to Golly I knew!"

CHAPTER V

Dinner for Two

THE dining room of the Abbott House, Abbottsville's largest and swankiest hotel, would have done credit to the Lido. Not as to size, but as to atmosphere and appointment. Tables were set far apart, sheltered from each other by potted palms, so that the occupants of one were more or less discreetly shielded from a party at another. A small fountain tinkled at the far end of the room, bathed by a hundred colored lights, and above it, on a dais, a discreet salon orchestra of piano, violin and cello held forth softly and melodiously. The entrance itself was a wide flight of seven marble stairs, shielded from the lobby by a heavy black velvet drape, rich and full.

The usual smattering of citizens partially filled the room tonight. Among them, Luke Melton, proprietor of the Southern Club, sat about half-way down the room on the right, where his view of the entrance was unobscured by palms, or fellow diners. Melton was fifty-five years old, a man of distinguished appearance, perhaps a bit narrow between the eyes, but whose graying hair and well-cut clothes indicated him as a person of success, manners and breeding. With him sat Amos Carter, owner and publisher of the *Courier*.

Carter was tall and cadaverous, with the affected manners and actions of an old school thespian. He wore his hair long, he talked so vehemently that from time to time it fell across his eyes. His collar was high and winged, he wore a stock rather than a tie. He was an odd companion for a man of the world, suave and assured, like Luke Melton.

Against the opposite wall, but in plain sight of the Melton table, dined three heavily-set men, unmistakable as to their calling. Mayor John Chambers could h a v e but one nickname—Honest John. He was typical politician, from his ample g i r t h to his pink cheeks and his several chins. With him was Carson Thames, chief of police of Abbottsville, almost as heavy as the mayor, but not quite so paunchy. A heavy, bristling moustache overhung his petulant upper lip, his eyes were cold and unforgiving. Here was a man that thought a lot of his own abilities and despised those so-called abilities in anyone else. The third in the party was young Doctor Rudolph Blitz, a protege of Mayor Chambers. Already Doctor Blitz was doing well in Abbottsville. He was, as a matter of fact, the medical examiner, as well as the supervisor of public health, and holder of several other appointive offices.

At the first mentioned table, Carter, the newspaper editor, held forth on some lengthy subject to Melton, the gambler. Melton let the cadaverous one talk, simply nodded from time to time, seemed to scarcely pay any attention. Occasionally, as his eyes strayed to the curtained entrance, he glanced at a wafer thin watch.

Of the three at the second table, only Thames, the chief of police, was silent. The other two seemed wrapped

> To whom it may concern:
>
> I would like to say something nice about Dr. Harker's Chickasha Remedies, but unfortunately I did not consider them soon enough.
>
> (signed) Luigi Maroni

in a jovial discussion of something or other. Oddly enough, it was Thames, the chief of police, who duplicated Melton's feat of constantly eyeing the velvet drapes that shielded the entrance, constantly glancing at his own wrist watch.

The three-piece salon orchestra rendered a Strauss waltz with feeling. The velvet curtains at the h e a d of the marble stairs parted. For a m o m e n t a woman stood there, alone, the dark drapes forming a background for her exquisite perfection. She was tall and she was imperious, from her severely coiffured hair to the tips of silver slippers that barely peeped from beneath the folds of the moulded, white velvet evening gown. That hair was black as a raven's wing, and as shiny. The eyes were widely spaced, slightly slanting. The face was heart-shaped, the solitary touch of color a slash of deep crimson that was her mouth. The gown was daring, extremely decollete, yet she wore it with an air that made it suitable. At her slender waist she wore a solitary orchid.

Here was a woman, a casual observer might note, who was born to evening clothes. Watching her, seeing her stand there proud and imperiously, sweeping the room indolently and appraisingly through those oriental eyes, you could no more imagine her in— say a gingham house dress—than a Menjou in overalls.

The curtain behind her parted and the contrast was startling. Luigi Maroni, beaming fatuously, stood beside her. Maroni was resplendent in tails and a white tie. The bosom of his shirt made the swarthiness of his heavy face more pronounced than ever. Maroni was a big man. Not fat, but huge. He weighed, perhaps, two hundred and fifty pounds, and not an ounce of that poundage was excess fat. He put his hairy fingers possessively on the white arm of the woman, the twist of his lips was meant for a smile. She turned, she smiled up at him, she raised her long skirt slightly with her left hand, and together they came down the steps.

The gambler, Melton, sat back in his chair and sighed deeply, his eyes on the woman. Maroni saw him, grinned triumphantly, lifted a hand. Melton nodded, turned back to the raving and ranting of Carter, the newspaper publisher.

But Police Chief Carson Thames was not the poker faced gambler. He arose so abruptly he almost overturned his chair. His already florid face turned a deeper red; his moustache bristled like the hackles of a dog. Growling deep in his throat, he hurried forward to intercept the couple, who had been met by an obsequious head waiter as they reached the bottom of the wide stairs.

The smile on Maroni's face turned to a scowl. He interposed his bulk between the police chief and the cool beauty at his side.

Thames growled, "Lita, you owe me an explanation at least. You begged off. You said you were ill—"

Maroni put his hand on Thames' chest, pushed him so that he went backward three steps to keep from falling. "Listen," snarled Maroni, "whenever Lita owes explanations to a guy like you—"

"Please," said the woman called Lita. And it was hard to tell whether it was

pleasure, derision, or scorn that made that peculiar light in her slanting eyes.

Even at that Thames would undoubtedly have sprung at the larger man had it not been for young Blitz, who leaped after him and caught his arm. Honest John Chambers hurried up, beaming, as if this byplay of seething emotions was something to be expected and merely overlooked.

"Miss Bane, Miss Bane, you're lovely tonight! And Mr. Maroni! Ah, you young dogs have all the luck!" He shook hands ostentatiously with Maroni, who still glowered at the red-faced Thames. "And Miss Bane, may I introduce Doctor Blitz? Doctor Blitz, Miss Lita Bane."

Miss Bane's throaty voice said that she had seen the doctor several times at the Southern Club. "I trust your practise is more successful than your gambling," she said, and looked away, uninterested.

The mayor invited them to join his party. Maroni said stiffly they preferred to dine alone. The white shoulders of Miss Lita Bane proclaimed that it made no difference to her whether she dined alone, or in a group.

THE Strauss waltz had changed to Debussy when the curtains parted again. Hercules Jones, resplendent in a dinner coat, stood there, holding the curtains aside. So wide was his chest that his exposed white shirt might well have been calculated in acres rather than inches. He was scrubbed to pink perfection, and it would have been hard to believe that only a short while ago this same behemoth was laying face downward in a puddle of rainwater outside the rear garages of the Resthaven Courts!

But Doctor Harker! True, he still wore a Prince Albert coat; he was still dressed as he had been when the red coupe pulled the boxlike trailer into Abbottsville. Perhaps it was the surroundings that heightened his appearance, the dark curtain that emphasized the silver whiteness of his hair, the elegance of his flowing moustache and nicely trimmed goatee.

His eyes swept over the room. Doctor Harker was a poker player par excellence, as well as a master phychologist. He knew his entrance was dramatic, his appearance, with Herk Jones as a foil, extraordinary. And his senses were trained finely enough to note any change of expression, no matter how small. To himself, after the one sweeping glance, he was saying: Chambers, Thames and a man I don't know, Melton, Carter, Maroni and *Brenda Sloan.*

Carter, the newspaper man, after one brief glance, had resumed his harangue, his eyes turned from the doctor. Melton, the gambler, stared at them blankly. So might he have stared at the waiter, or the fountain, or the musicians, with his mind on a thousand other things. Thames, still angry, glared. Chambers beamed. The stranger, who was Blitz, smiled in derision.

Doc Harker heard Hercules expell his breath in a long sigh of rapture. He turned quickly, saw the big man's eyes fixed on the slender, exotic figure of the woman who sat with the man, Maroni. "Gee," said Herk, deep in his chest, as if the sight of her choked him up, and "Gee!"

A waiter approached. Doc Harker tread heavily on Herk's number twelve. Herk said, "Ouch!" He turned red beneath Harker's accusing gaze, followed him like a great dog—meekly—until they were opposite the Maroni table. There, unable to help himself, he slowed, beaming.

Maroni was angry anyway. He pushed back his chair, he stood up. He was larger even than Herk Jones. Herk was so rapturous he was jittery. Had he possessed a tail it would have been wagging at a great rate. Lita Bane stared down demurely at her cocktail glass. Herk looked puzzled.

Maroni said—and it took but seconds for all this to happen— "Listen, are you trying to kiss in, too? Do you want—" He laid his big hand against Hercules' white shirt bosom and pushed. Nothing happened except that Maroni went back a couple of steps.

"Hey," said Hercules, to Lita Bane. "Aw gee whiz—" Then the doctor had him by the arm. But not before Maroni, somewhat startled by the Gibralter firmness of the man, stepped in quickly, and, already angered by Carson Thames' attitude, started a right hook. Started, because Hercules simply moved his great chin the fraction of an inch, caught the wrist of the fist a it whistled by.

"Now, now," chided Doctor Harker, "Hercules, you've made a mistake! Now, now!"

Maroni was bending inward at the knees, a look of utter consternation on his face as his wrist was crushed in those steel fingers. Doctor Harker brought his heel down viciously on Herk's instep, twisted.

Herk said, "Ouch!" He released the wrist.

Maroni straightened. For a moment it was a toss-up whether he would swing his left, or nurse his right. The right won. He stepped back, wrapped his left hand around the sore wrist and spoke feelingly and well.

Doc Harker caught Herk again by the sleeve. His suave voice spoke to Lita Lane and to Maroni. "Please accept my most humble apologies. No doubt, my assistant thought he recognized one of you. Hercules, tell the lady and the gentleman that you're sorry."

He was slightly behind the towering Hercules Jones. His forefinger went delicately to his right temple, he rolled his eyes, looked appealingly at Maroni. A look of understanding came over Maroni's tough features. He nodded to Doc Harker.

Herk, a bit bewildered, was saying, "—and I sure beg your pardon, ma'am. It's only that you look like a babe I knew back home and—"

Doc Harker led him away, still muttering. Maroni sat down. Lita Bane shrugged beautiful shoulders, picked up her cocktail glass. Sitting down himself, Harker saw Maroni speak to her, saw her shrug again. Sullenly, Herk took a chair, held by the waiter. Sullenly because he knew what was coming.

The waiter hovered, the menus were in place. Doc Harker waved him away. The doctor's smile was beatific, but his eyes were venomous on his big assistant. "I believe," he said, "we'll just move these flowers, my lame brained friend."

He arose, picked up the vase of flowers that ornamented their table, moved three quick strides to the next table and sat it down. Returning, he glanced at the flowers. A small bullseye mirror with a spring clip was partially concealed by the blossoms. In it, he could make out the table where sat the mayor, Chambers, Thames, the chief of police, and the man he did not know, who was Doctor Blitz, the Mayor's protege. The other tables which interested him, he could see from his own chair.

He twirled his moustaches, beamed at Hercules. "Of all the unmitigated, unqualified, consummate jackasses I ever saw, Hercules, you are the worst." A watcher might have thought he was asking the big man whether he preferred a soup or a cocktail. Herk turned redder. Sullenly he answered, "Now what'd I do? You said maybe we'd see Brenda. We see Brenda, I start to speak to her and—what the hotel?"

"Exactly," said the doctor, smiling, eventually breaking into a high-pitched laugh, as if Hercules had told him a great joke. He glanced at the bullseye mirror, saw the black, brooding, suspicious eyes of Carson Thames ,fixed upon them. He said, "It was like this." And from his pocket he drew an envelope—and a pencil. While his lips said one thing, his pencil wrote, "Never mind now, don't mention the name Brenda, but wait until I get you home."

"Now do you understand?" he beamed.

And Hercules Jones, who understood none of it, smiled and said he understood perfectly.

GUESTS came and went. The doctor ate well. Hercules Jones, in spite of his sullenness and his fear of the wrath to come, ate enormously. There was a little matter of a double T-bone with a double order of French fries and a plate of beans. This vanished like paraphenalia in a prestidigitator's act. The wide-eyed waiter brought the second steak and the fourth cup of coffee. Eleven hard rolls disappeared into the big man's maw. At last, he pushed back his chair and sighed heavily.

The doctor observed him with magnanimity. "It is remarkable to me," he said, beaming and smiling, "how a man with a head so appallingly solid can possess a body so hollow."

Herk sulked. "Lookit," he expostulated, "how was I to know? Like I was telling you coming into this jerkwater town, if you'd let us in on your plans! How was I to know that Brenda was under cover again—"

"Ssssh!" The doctor's blue veined hand came up in warning. Across the room he could see Carter, the newspaper publisher and Melton, the gambler, observing them keenly. Now one of Doctor Thaddeus Harker's many accomplishments was lip reading. This often times aided him greatly.

For example, now, he knew that Carter, the publisher, was saying, "As obviously phony as a celluloid collar!" And that Melton, the gambler, replied, "Carter, that is your trouble. You look for and believe in the obvious too much, which is the reason you're such a poor card player. Doesn't it ever occur to you that—take the little goat for example. Don't you think he might *want* to look like a phony?"

Doc Harker arose, leaving Herk open mouthed at the table. In his hand he bore a handful of cards, his own personal cards. At every table he paused to bow, to murmur, "Allow me," and to lay a card at each elbow. Guests picked these cards up—they were the double variety, folding in the middle—and observed them with laughter. When he arrived at the table of the gambler and Carter, he said, "Gentlemen, I take it from your conversation that you are puzzled as to my identity." Two cards took their proper places. Then the little doctor was gone, leaving Melton as blank faced as ever, but leaving Carter open-mouthed as he picked up the card.

By now the mayor, the chief of police, Blitz, all had a card. So quickly had Doc Harker moved that no one had stopped him. Now, as he laid cards at the elbows of Lita Bane and Maroni,

a waiter hurried forward to whisper discreetly in his ear. Greatly insulted, his moustaches fairly bristling, the doctor went back to his table. "I think," he said majestically, "that we shall go, Hercules. This man objects to my introducing myself—"

"Now look," said the waiter, worried, "it's not me. It's just a rule, see?"

"Quite," said the doctor, "and to show there are no hard feelings—" He took a pencil from the waiter's pocket, picked up a menu, scrawled *Thaddeus Clay Harker* across it. "My autograph," he said. He headed for the door, Herk lumbering after him. At the top of the steps he paused, to survey the room majestically. Practically every eye was upon him. It was the kind of exit the doctor liked. The limelight! He bowed, in courtly manner, went through the curtain. Hercules could not resist temptation. He raised both hands above his head and clasped them, in the manner of a fighter introduced to a crowd.

But in the lobby he laid a hand on the doctor's shoulder. "Lookit," he began aggrievedly, "how's Brenda going to know where we are at, or us know where she's at?"

Doctor Harker, who was headed for the cigar stand, shook off his hand wordlessly. He bought a handful of his favorite cheap black stogies, blew smoke at Hercules, who promptly dodged backward. A colored bellboy came over, said, "Doctor Thaddeus Harker, suh?" The doctor acknowledged his identity.

"Theah's a gentleman in the Blue Room, suh, waiting for you, please suh?"

"Thank you," said the doctor and drew a cardboard disc from his pocket. He handed it to the bellboy. The disc read, "This entitles bearer to one bottle Doctor Harker's Chickasha Remedy." He headed for the Blue Room.

Carson Thames, chief of police, did not arise, nor did he wave his visitor to a chair. He observed the immaculate, little doctor through heavy lids, and said, "You're staying at Resthaven, aren't you, pitchman?"

The doctor said nothing.

"You know who I am?"

"Carson Thames, chief of police of Abbottsville. Formerly a policeman in New York City, broken for drinking on duty, accused of taking graft, accusation never proven, brought before the board in November '29, negligence of duty, suspicion of cowardice in allowing loft robbers to—"

Thames was on his feet, his face livid. He raised his first as if to strike the smaller man. The veins in his forehead were like whipcords, his eyes were blazing. "You—you—" he began. And stopped.

Hercules Jones stepped into the room, said, "Trouble, doc?" He looked like he hoped there was trouble. He looked like he was made for trouble.

"Why, no, Hercules," said the doctor slowly. "You wanted to see me, Mr. Thames, or should I say—chief?"

Slowly, Thames gained control of himself. The red receded from his features and he breathed less noisily through his nose. He took the doctor's double card from his pocket, tore it contemptuously in two ways and tossed it to the floor. He said, "I'm giving you until morning to get out of town, Harker. We don't allow peddlers and pitchman in Abbottsville."

Harker answered softly, "You mistake me, Chief, you mistake me. I am not here to make a pitch. As a matter of fact, we intend taking a course of baths, my assistant and myself. There are, I trust, no objections to that?"

And before Thames could answer he turned and stalked out the door. In the lobby the same colored bellhop approached. "A gemmun left this for you, suh," he said, and put a folded piece of menu in Doctor Harker's hand. He hurried away before the doctor could fumble another free bottle of *Chickasha Remedies* from his pocket.

The piece of menu bore writing, which read: "Southern Club, before midnight. Your own advantage. Melton."

He placed it carefully in his pocket, strode through the lobby, oblivious of the fact that all eyes were upon him, went out the door, Herk at his elbow. A careful observer might have noted a new and springier elasticity to the little doctor's step. Since coming to Abbottsville things were decidedly picking up. The doctor liked action. He was getting it. But why, he asked himself, did the name, Thaddeus Harker, inspire such action?

The red coupe was parked at the curb. Herk unlocked it, got in, the doctor following. Someone tapped on the window. Doctor Harker rolled it down slightly, peered into the earnest face of the man he did not know, the man who had dined with Honest John Chambers and Chief of Police Thames.

He said, whispering carefully, though Doc Harker's quick look showed that there was no one else about, "Should I tell him you're here? Where should he meet you?"

"I am afraid," said the little doctor stiffly, "that I do not have the pleasure of your acquaintance, sir. To whom do you refer?"

"Listen I'm Rudolph Blitz, son-in-law to Arthur Wallace. Should I tell him you're here? Do you want to see him?"

"I think," said the doctor coolly,

"that you are laboring under a misapprehension. Drive on, Hercules, drive on."

Hercules drove on. The rain had ceased.

───────

CHAPTER VI

Take a Walk, Doc

HERCULES JONES was exceedingly angry. Hercules would readily admit that o r d i n a r y closeness· of mouth was, on occasions a very good and even a very necessary thing. But, he maintained, it could be carried too far. Nothing Doc Harker did, nothing that had happened to them, since approaching Abbottsville, made any sense. And Doctor Harker, rather than trusting his assistant, merely looked mysterious and smiled, like a skunk on a garbage pail, as Hercules likened him, or else gnawed one of his moustachios and glared, lifting a blue-veined hand for silence.

"First," Hercules summed up bitterly, "you won't tell me just why we're here, what we got in mind. I *know* we didn't come all these miles just to make a pitch. Next we run into that monkey Stanley, who must be a red hot—"

"Or a detective, perhaps a G-man," put in Thaddeus Harker softly.

Hercules started. G-man! Copper! He hadn't plumbed those possibilities.

"And then," he persisted, "I get smacked in the sconce, all my pockets is gone through and my keys tooken, and this here Stanley shows up missing, even if he is dead with a wire around his neck! Now I ask you, did he drive away? And I tell you, no! But will you let me stay and find Georgie, on account of I think it was Georgie smacked me?"

He wheeled the car indignantly around the corner. The doctor lit one of his black stogies and looked benevolent.

"No," griped Hercules, his lower lip lengthening, "you keep it all to yourself, and why, I ask you, why? You knew all those guys at the cafe! We saw Brenda and she pretended like she didn't know me. Who was the mug she was with? It may be I want to look him up." He scowled darkly. "And how about that four-eyed monkey that come out to the car?"

The coupe filled with the thick, nauseating smoke. Hercules coughed. The doctor said, "You may pull up here, Hercules." Hercules tooled the coupe in to the curb with one hand. The other was rolling down the window. Doctor Harker opened the door. He slammed the door. Hercules immediately opened it and began fanning at the smelly smoke with both hands.

Doctor Thaddeus Harker nodded magnanimously at the startled soda clerk. He asked the druggist ceremoniously if it would be quite all right if he used the phone. The druggist waved at the booth, growled something about having a nickel, and went back to his crossword puzzle.

A few seconds later, Thaddeus Harker said in a modulated voice, "I should like to speak to Mr. Arthur Wallace, please."

At the other end of the phone there was a moment of hesitation. Then, "And who wishes to speak to Mr. Wallace, please?"

"Doctor Thaddeus Clay Harker."

He waited, impatiently. Through the dirty glass of the booth he could see an advertising clock above the front door. It said eight-fifty. Time ticked on. He jiggled the hook. The operator informed him coldly that he was still connected with his number. Doctor Harker begged her pardon profusely.

"Hello, hello, Thad?" The voice was scarcely a whisper, low and hoarse. The little doctor stiffened. "This is Harker," he answered cautiously. "What's wrong, Arthur?"

"Cold," whispered Arthur, in answer. "Influenza."

For moments they talked, Harker carrying on for the greater portion of the time. Wallace, claiming to have been in bed several days, asked the doctor to wait until tomorrow to see him, as he was supposed to have no visitors.

"Oh—ah—Arthur, and about that little matter of which you wrote me a month ago?"

Arthur laughed hollowly. "Thad, I'm going to be truthful with you—I guess I'm an alarmist. Afterward, when I thought over that letter to you I was heartily ashamed of myself. I'll tell you all about it tomorrow."

Cautiously Harker said, "Then the little matter of which you spoke so feelingly needs no attention, Arthur?"

"The little matter," said Arthur Wallace, "has been attended to. I mentioned my son-in-law, Dr. Blitz, in that letter, didn't I?" Harker agreed that he did. "Doctor Blitz simply went to the men responsible for that condition of which I spoke, and talked eloquently. And Thad, I will tell you what I will do. You can look Abbottsville over from outskirts to outskirts, and for every wanted criminal you find, I shall reward you with a—quart of that scotch you love so well."

Doctor Harker was properly delighted at this disclosure by his old friend. He murmured something about calling on Wallace the first thing tomorrow, trusting he would spend a

fine and restful night, and hung up. But he did not leave the booth at once. Instead he applied an old fashioned match to the dead stogie, leaned back in the booth and reflected.

There was, he decided, something decidedly wrong. In the first place, Arthur Wallace, in the old days, had always called him by a nickname, Warsaw. This, no doubt, from Porter's book of their youth, Thaddeus of Warsaw. True, he used the name Thaddeus in their correspondence, but that was more or less of a serious, down-to-earth enterprise. Would he, then, shift from "Warsaw" to "Thad," something he had never used before in conversation? Would he offer to bet a bottle of scotch whiskey when he must of necessity know that Doctor Thaddeus Harker was practically raised on bourbon, when, as a matter of fact, from time to time, on holidays and birthdays, he had sent a case—not of scotch —but of bourbon to his old friend?

But, most of all, could a leopard change his spots over night? Could all the so-called immune criminals be forced to leave Abbottsville over night simply because the crooked politicians or policemen, who encouraged their presence, saw the light of civic virtue? Either, concluded Doc Harker, his friend Arthur Wallace had grown senile and addled, or something was screwy.

The door of the booth suddenly jerked open, a heavy hand reached in and grasped the doctor's shoulder, dragged him unceremoniously forth. It was the druggist. "In there, in there," he screeched, and the soda clerk, fire extinguisher, upended, sprayed the inside of the booth with chemical.

Doctor Harker, shaking lose in the excitement, adjusted his white hat and went out the door, believing flight wiser than lengthy explanations. He did, however, toss the stogie in the still wet gutter before climbing into the red coupe.

"The Southern Club," he said briefly, and Hercules, still stubborn, pulled away from the curb.

THE Southern Club made no pretense of being other than it was, a gambling establishment. There was, however, a small bar, well-appointed, just past the check room, where a man might pause for encouragement before passing through the heavily-draped doorway that led to the gaming rooms, or stop for consolation on the way out. There Doctor Harker, still turning the Wallace puzzle over and over in his mind, called for the bourbon bottle. Hercules, still pouting, drank soda.

From behind the drapes came the babble of many voices. The door to the gambling room released a man. The light gleamed on the yellow waves of his hair. Hercules stiffened. He actually growled far back in his throat. He said, "Georgie!" and started forward. Doc Harker's small hand held him back. But it couldn't hold back the rumblings in the ex-wrestler's chest.

Georgie Vasey stood in the doorway while he lighted a cigarette. He came past the doctor and Hercules on his softly treading feet. He slowed. He looked at Hercules' belt buckle for the space of five full seconds, nodded briefly and went on out the front door.

"Lookit," rumbled Hercules, "six, two and even I will bet he was the guy what crowned me! Lookit, quick, doc, before he gets away! Let me put the pressure on him and find out what happened to the coupe and the sedan and the dead guy!"

Harker kicked his shin viciously.

The bartender stood almost opposite them polishing glasses, and Hercules, angry and excited was not apt to use a whispering tone. But if the bartender noticed the words, his face did not show it. He continued to gaze into the distance and slide the towel about the thin cocktail glass.

Harker nodded toward him, kicked at Hercules again, missed, filled his glass for the second time. The door to the gambling room opened again. A small man, as small as the doctor, swarthy-faced, sporting a toothbrush moustache as black as his eyes and hair, moved up to the bar. Wordlessly, the bartender set out a bottle of Vermouth, a bottle of bitters.

The front door opened. The uniformed doorman thrust in his head. To the bartender he said, "Hey, find out who owns this red fire wagon. The cop on the beat says it'll have to be moved. The monkey parked by a fireplug."

Doctor Thaddeus Harker looked at the bewildered Hercules and sighed. "Lookit, doc," disclaimed the big man, "if there's a fire plug where we parked the city just put it in. I tell you—"

"See about it, Hercules," said the doctor, and refilled his glass. Looking like an aggrieved child, Hercules went out the door. Before it closed another man entered. He, too, was sallow-faced; he, too, wore a black, toothbrush moustache.

The doctor drank his whiskey, laid a bill on the bar. The newcomer took his place at the doctor's left. They stared in the mirror at the doctor. The bartender moved away discreetly, pursed his fat lips in a whistle, stared off into space. At least *he* didn't mean to see anything.

Doctor Harker said gravely, "What will it be, boys?"

"A walk," said the newcomer, and something bored into the little doctor's left kidney, something hard and unyielding. He winced. But the hand he reached for the whiskey bottle was steady. In spite of the gun he filled his glass once more, never spilling a drop. "Sir," he said gravely, "the gun is no threat whatsoever. You wouldn't dare shoot me here and I have no intentions of anything except going for the walk you mentioned. I am, however, an advocate of good bourbon. This happens to be good. We shall proceed shortly."

He drank again.

"Wise guy," snorted the man with the gun. "Now move. You don't need to hang back hoping for the big ox. He's being taken care of."

Doctor Harker drew a linen handkerchief almost as large as a bed sheet from his pocket, wiped his lips, his moustache, his goatee carefully. In the mirror he adjusted his hat, his string tie, smoothed his lapels. But, to his surprise, instead of being led out the front door, he followed the first man through the doorway beside that which led to the gambling room! Jauntily he whistled an air, Spanish American War vintage, as they went down the hallway. Another man, also sallow as to face, black as to toothbrush moustache, sat on a divan before a blank door. He stared at the tips of his shoes, after favoring them with one glance.

CHAPTER VII

Finders Keepers

THE door opened, after a brief knock and a muffled word. Doctor Harker walked into the office. He took off his hat, bowed magnanimously, said, "Luke Melton, I believe? Though I have not had the pleasure—"

"Sit down, Doctor Harker," said Luke Melton, and to the others, "Thank you, boys. You can go."

The door closed. Doctor Harker said, "I take it that someone is holding a gun on me, Mr. Melton. You didn't ask the boys if I was armed."

"Right, Doctor Harker," replied Luke Melton. He leaned back in his swivel chair, placed the tips of his fingers together and regarded the doctor as one might regard a strange animal. "Doctor," he said calmly, "you interest me."

"So much so," nodded Harker, "that you ask me to call on you, and when I am in the process of so doing, you send men with guns to meet me, to bring me to you. Hardly consistant, Mr. Melton."

Melton said, "Considering what has happened, Doctor, you can hardly blame me. You see, when I sent you the note, I didn't know all that had occurred."

Doctor Harker bowed politely. "I wonder," he said gravely, "if you will allow me to ask a few questions before we get down to business? In that manner I may better know what to answer. For I presume it is information of one sort, or another, that you are after?"

"Questions," said Melton, "are hardly necessary, Doctor. Perhaps I can tell you a bit of a tale that will do away with the questions?"

"May I?" asked the doctor. At Melton's nod, he drew forth another of the stogies, applied the old fashioned lucifer and leaned back as if ready to listen to an adventure story from a crony in his own social club.

"I won't go into your past, Doctor," started Melton. "Suffice to say that I have investigated you thoroughly, that I know you are one of the major scientific criminologists of the country, in spite of your eccentric appearance, in spite of—ah—your profession."

Doctor Thaddeus Harker nodded, pleased, evidently.

"Yes, as soon as I learned that Arthur Wallace wrote you requesting help in cleaning up Abbottsville, I looked you up." Now, no doubt Luke Melton expected Doc Harker to show surprise when he evinced this piece of information. Doc Harker's face simply kept its blandness, yet inwardly he was duly noting the statement: *Melton knew Wallace had written him.*

"As a matter of fact," went on Melton, "that letter imploring your help was absolutely unnecessary. It may be that in the past, Abbottsville was a bit lenient with those who walk the shady paths. But believe me, Doctor, we were not unaware of the fact that we were sitting on the edge of a volcano. Consequently, through the offices of the *Courier,* aided by the chief of police, and all prominent citizens, we were enabled to rid ourselves of the cuckoo's egg, to get rid of the criminal element that infested Abbottsville. The town is now clean."

"So I understand from Mr. Wallace." Melton's brows went up. "I talked to him on the phone not long ago."

Melton nodded. "You understand, then?"

"I understand. I understand that you gentlemen who run Abbottsville do not care for my presence particularly. That since there is nothing to clean up there is no point in my lingering."

> To whom it may concern:
>
> Dr. Harker's Chickasha Remedies helped change the entire course of my life—and also my brother's. Thanks to Dr. Harker.
>
> (signed) Jeannie Wright

"That," said Melton, "was the situation up until earlier this evening. You know, of course, what has altered that situation Doctor?" The doctor raised his brows. "Come, come, Doctor, give me credit for a little sense. Let me tell you this. As you came into Abbottsville it so happened that you ran into a gentleman with a flat tire."

It was hard now for Doctor Harkness to keep his face bland and expressionless. A gentleman with a flat tire. A gentleman who was fired at from a speeding sedan. A gentleman who met death with a wire garrotte about his throat, whose corpse disappeared from the Resthaven tourist camp!

"You aided and assisted this gentleman, Doctor. At least your man did. Now I would very much like to get in touch with this man, Mr.—"

"Stanley," said the doctor gravely, "A cosmetic salesman, I believe."

The mask faded from Melton's face. It contorted with anger. He leaned forward and slapped the desk. "Harker," he grated, "you'll never get away with this. You were the last man to see—ah —Stanley, you and that ox of yours! Stanley never got to Abbottsville, where he had a very definite appointment!"

Harker raised his hand. His voice was cold now, his moustaches bristling. "Stanley means nothing to me. As far as I know he was a cosmetic salesman. But, few cosmetic salesmen carry shoulder guns and have bullet-proof glass in their cars. Let's name names—Stanley was—"

"All right," snapped Melton, "Stanley is Shag Zachary, recently released from the Federal penetentiary. Now, Harker, where is he?"

Harker shrugged. Musingly he said, "No wonder I didn't recognize him. Zachary, the brain. The man who was clever enough to remain Mr. Anonymous, who stayed out of the papers, stayed behind the scenes! No, I don't feel badly about failing to recognize him! Not at all! I don't suppose a dozen citizens in the United States knew what Shag Zachary really looks like!"

Melton snapped, "Never mind your soliloquies! I want to know where Shag Zachary is! You're the last man to have definitely seen him."

Harker regarded him gravely. His voice was gentle. "Be truthful, Melton. The set-up is too obvious. For years, you fellows run a town like Abbottsville, a cooling off spot for criminals. Suddenly you go pure, you reform, you get rid of your riffraff. Why? Because something big is coming up. You don't want to run a chance of investigation. What is that something big? Shag Zachary. Now Shag Zachary doesn't show up and you tear your hair. Why, Melton? Zachary has spent eleven years in prison. It would be impossible for him to take up in the rackets where he left off! You don't give a hoot about Zachary himself. Just what was he bringing that made him so important to you?"

Melton gazed long and intently at the little pitchman. He smiled, "Since it can't possibly matter, just to let you know where you stand," he smiled, "Shag Zachary was bringing nine hundred thousand dollars worth of securities and bonds to Abbottsville to be disposed of. Doctor Harker, knowing you and your reputation, I am convinced that you either have Shag

Zachary, or you have those securities."

"And where would I have them, my dear sir?"

"In the safe on wheels that you have parked at the Resthaven camp. Oh, I've had a man looking at it, Doctor. A good crib man. He says it can't be opened without dynamite or soup. So, suppose you and I and a couple of my boys take a ride to Resthaven. Suppose you're good enough to show us how to take that trailer apart, a board and a bolt at a time. Suppose—"

THE door flew open. A woman's hysterical voice shrilled, "You'll get back there and keep your hands off me, or I'll shoot, damn you. I'll kill you!"

Jeannie Wright came into the room, leaned against the door as she closed it behind her in the guard's anxious face. Her own face was so white that her rouged cheeks gave her the appearance of a circus clown. Her eyes were wide and staring, light danced off the gleaming array of her hair. The gun she held on Melton, however, was steady.

Melton half arose, the gun waved him back. "Damn you, damn you," she grated, hysteria tingeing her voice, "where is he? What have you done with him?"

"Now Jeannie," soothed the gambler, keeping his features calm, "there's no reason to be so upset. He's simply delayed and—"

"My last wire was from St. Joseph, forty-two miles down the line. He should have covered it in less than an hour, he should have gotten in around four. It's ten now. Something's happened, there's been a leak, and I mean to know where and why!"

Nearer and nearer she came to Melton. The knuckle of her trigger finger tightened. "I told him not to trust any of you cheap two-by-four crooks," she snarled. "If something's happened to him, after I've waited all these years—if—oh!"

A hairy hand reached through velvet hangings, a hairy hand that grasped a heavy Lüger. The gun rose and fell sharply across the woman's wrist. Her gun dropped to the floor. Again she cried out with the pain of the blow. Moving like a cat, Melton scooped up her gun, covered Doctor Harker, who had gotten to his feet and was half across the office.

"Hold it," he said grimly, and the doctor bowed, smiled. To the woman he said, "You're absolutely right, Jeannie. Something has happened. What, I don't know, but I mean to find out and I can't be bothered now with a hysterical woman." He held aside a part of the drape, continued, "In there, Jeannie. Take her, mister. Keep her there until I get back."

The same hairy hand reached out and grasped the woman's shoulder, wisped her through the slot in the hangings. The curtain dropped into place.

"Thank you, Mr. Melton," said Doctor Harker courteously. "You've saved me a bit of trouble. Mrs.—ah—Wright didn't quite ring true to me, so I obtained her prints, meaning to have them checked. Now it won't be at all necessary."

"No? To hell with that, Doctor. What do you think she is?"

"I seem to recall," said the doctor mildly, "that Shag Zachary had a sister very devoted to him. And her name was—ah—Jean."

Melton shrugged. "We're going," he said flatly, "to open that safe on wheels, my friend. Suppose you get going? We'll pick up a couple of boys in the bar."

Doctor Harker smiled. He said, "Really, Melton, you under-estimate us. If you will bother to look behind you, you will note Hercules Jones at the window, with a very large gun in his hand, a tommy gun, aimed, I believe, right directly at the middle of your back."

Melton said, "Not this time, Doctor. That one's too old."

Glass tinkled. As Melton half turned toward the window, Doctor Harker moved amazingly fast for one so apparently aged. He snatched the ashtary from the floor, brought it down across Melton's hand. Melton's gun exploded, the bullet plowed a furrow in the carpet. The curtain jerked aside. A man leaped into the room, a Lüger in his hand. Hot eyes shot about the room, saw the broken window. The Lüger dropped from his hairy fingers, very slowly he raised his hands shoulder high, glared accusingly at Luke Melton, whose hands likewise were going up.

Doctor Harker said, "We meet again, Chief Thames." And to the man in the window, "Do come in, Hercules, it must be uncomfortable out there in the mud. And where did you get the nice tommy-gun?"

Hercules Jones raised the broken window, stepped in, grinning.

"Lookit, doc," he crowed, patting the gun stock. "Always I wanted me one of these and now I got one! Where'd I get it? Lookit, doc, I practically found it! A guy poked it in my kidney! So I took it away from him!"

Doctor Harker smiled, as one might smile at a precocious child. "Finders keepers," he said primly. "Now, Hercules, if you'll restrain these gentlemen until I get—ah—Miss Zachary—from the other room, we'll take a ride."

CHAPTER VIII

Death Across the Hall

THERE were times when Brenda Sloan found her job as undercover agent for Doctor Thaddeus Clay Harker more than a little irksome. Doctor Harker, to begin with, was inordinately close-mouthed, which sometimes rankled. Was it because he didn't trust her? True, he sent her places; he told her not only what he wanted to know, but exactly how to learn those things. But he never gave her a *Why*, which, considering the makeup of all women, pretty or ugly, was extremely provoking.

For four weeks Brenda Sloan had lived in an expensive suite at the Abbott House, under the name of Lita Bane. She had dressed exotically; she had given the general aura of a woman of mystery. Mail had arrived for her from the four quarters of the nation; mail, which on being read by a curious outsider, could be deciphered to mean almost anything. She drove an expensive car. She gambled. She did not plunge; she did not excite curiosity by her great means. She was, to all appearances, simply one Lita Bane, who knew her way about. A beautiful woman of the world, with some money, who in spite of her beauty, was evidently capable of looking out for Lita Bane.

But it was hard, hard to play this role, for Brenda Sloan was compassionate. She lacked the hard directness of Doctor Harker, whose makeup allowed no room for pity for a lawbreaker. There was a sense of pity in Brenda that persisted in bobbing up at the most inopportune moments. Tonight, for example.

She knew Luigi Maroni was bad,

knew he was as crooked as any man now doing time in Alcatraz. She knew he would steal and lie, knew he held his position here in this town of Abbottsville through fear. People feared him personally, his ruthlessness, his merciless ways. They feared the organization back of him, for, while Maroni posed as a contractor, the "workingmen" on his payroll never touched a pick or a hod or a hammer! They knew more about blackjacks and paper-wrapped, lead pipes. And—guns.

Nevertheless, in spite of these things, there was compassion in Lita's heart, pity for the man.

Maroni had been difficult all evening. The actions of Carson Thames had added fuel to the jealous fire that raged in his broad chest. The dumb show put on by Hercules Jones was more fuel. And the fact that she had allowed him to come here, to her apartment in the Abbott House; the fact that she had promised to answer his wild demands,—all of these things left him in a bad state as he paced the living room, while Brenda Sloan—alias Lita Bane—changed to lounging pajamas in the sanctity of her bedroom.

Four weeks, she mused, looking at her slim beauty in the glass, four weeks of this undercover business! She smiled wryly remembering the things Harker had demanded of her. She counted over the men she had met, purposely, on her slender fingers. She even reached into a drawer and drew forth a notebook, in which she had written a summation of character.

"Honest John Charmers: Hardly susceptible to feminine charm. A bag of wind. Either damnably dumb or damnably shrewd.

"Amos Carter: An out and out woman hater. Tried to get job on his paper, *The Courier*, informed coldly that he hired no women. Even his society editor is a man.

"Carson Thames: Very hot-blooded, accustomed to his own way always. Vain, egotistical and shrewd. A braggart. Boasted that he held the town in the hollow of his hand. A dangerous man.

"Luke Melton: The brains, undoubtedly, of the whole layout. Reads character, good psychologist, seems to see through me. All my obvious efforts to charm him are appreciated, yet met with a tongue-in-the-cheek.

"Maroni: The muscle!"

FROM the same drawer she took a pair of horn rimmed spectacles with colored lenses. They gave her a strange, owlish appearance. Her evening purse revealed the double card, garish and laughable, that had been laid at her elbow by Doctor Thaddeus Harker. The card was printed in red and black. One side read, "Doctor Thaddeus Clay Harker, God's Gift to Sufferers." And in red letters, on the opposite section, "Chickasha Remedies, Good for Man and Beast." The inside of the card was filled with a partial list of the ailments to be cured by Doctor Thadeus Harker's *Chickasha Remedies*. "Abcess, acariasis, acne, apepsia, beriberi, chilblain, dandruff, fibrositis, gastritis, halitosis, hangnail, heartburn, hypertension, lumbago, malaria, tapeworm, toothache, warts, wens."

Now this message was innocent enough in itself. But through the apparently innocent glasses, Brenda read Doctor Harker's message to her alone. It was written in marker's ink, well known to card sharks, available from any trick cardhouse. It said, "Resthaven. 34. Midnight. Careful." Those four words in Spencerian script, only those and nothing more.

Brenda looked at the French chime clock on her vanity. She had plenty of time. So, lighting a long cigarette, touching the lobes of her ears with perfume, she moved softly into the other room, where Luigi Maroni awaited her coming with hot eyes.

She smiled, moved to the portable bar, mixed two drinks. Her body cut off his view of the bar. Her drink was unnaturally light, his unnaturally heavy.

Even with his glass in his hand he could not take his eyes off her. Thickly he said, "Lita, there's no point in fooling around longer. I know I mean something to you, or you wouldn't throw Carson Thames over for me. For the last week you've been with no one but me."

Her smile was the smile of Lilith, enigmatic, leading.

He sat the glass down—empty—moved closer to where she stood, tried to take her hand. "Look Lita, and listen." His voice was husky with earnestness, and again a throb of conscience assailed her. "I'm not much, I've been rough and tough," he said earnestly. "I'm not in your class. I can't hold a candle to you for education and—well —manners and such. But ask anybody. Luigi Maroni is a money-maker. I can get you a nice home, I can get you plenty of clothes, and jewels and—and —everything a dame likes, I guess."

She forced herself to do it. She smiled at him, again that Mona Lisa smile. She shrugged. She said, "In Abbottsvillle?" With just the proper touch of scorn in her voice.

"No, by God," he roared, triumphantly, "not in Abbottsville! Another two or three days, not more than a week at most, and we can shake the dust of this hick town off our feet. Then its you and me, Lita, plenty of money, plenty of everything!"

Her eyes narrowed, she flicked the ash from her cigarette. "Luigi," she said softly, "let me tell you something." But first she mixed him another drink, put it into his anxious hands. "Luigi, I've been around. I've had a hard life, you can believe it, or not. All that I had, I had to get for myself. All that I ever lost, I lost because I believed some man. You promise a lot, and more than anything else in the world I want security. But—?" Again that shrug.

He drained his glass. He began to talk slowly. "I get it, honey. You don't trust me. You think I'm a bag of wind, like Thames! All right, listen. What would you say if I told you that within the next week I'll have nearly one hundred thousand dollars, of my own?"

That damnable shrug. "You don't believe it, hanh? Listen, did you ever hear of Shag Zachary?"

She nodded. He began to talk—and as he talked, his words gained impetus. They seemed to fairly rush and flow from his thick-lipped mouth, as if he had kept these plans, these secrets, too long in the great cave of his chest and they had spawned, multiplied and grown until his body was not of sufficient size to hold them any more.

She did two things for which she hated herself. She plied him with liquor and she dropped a word, or a query, deftly, from time to time, to lead him on. She hated herself for this because of one thing she was sure—Luigi Maroni might be a dangerous man; he might be cruel, a brute, an ex-thug, an exracketeer—but Luigi Maroni loved her. At least, he loved the woman he thought her to be.

AT ELEVEN o'clock she managed to somehow get his hat and topcoat on him. Maroni had drunk too much. But even at that, he seemed to realize that he had put his entire trust in the hands of his woman—and some seventh sense perhaps, warned him, that he had gone too far.

At the door, with the door open, he turned, to lean against the jamb. Thickly he said, "Aw right, aw right, you put me off again. Wanna tell you this, I love you, yes, but I know how to pay back the people that cross me. You know enough 'bout my plans now to do me dirt—but you ain't gonna do it, are you baby?"

She said, "Anything I know about you will go to the right parties, Luigi!"

He giggled a bit, cupped her chin with his huge hand. "Right parties, hanh babe, and the right parties is only us—you and me—and Shag Zachary! Rest of these birds think a man like Shag'd trust *them* when his old pal, Maroni, is 'round! Thas a laugh, a belly laugh."

He leaned and kissed her on the lips, his hat falling off as he did so. She pulled away quickly, murmured something or other, stepped inside and closed her door, leaning against it with sagging shoulders, the back of her hand pressed so hard against her rouged lips that her teeth broke skin.

Maroni obtained his hat, put it on, backwards. He straightened himself, took two steps down the hall with the high, careful steps of the inebriate. A voice called softly, "Hello, Maroni. How's things?"

Maroni's eyes shifted, circled, came to rest on the figure in the doorway opposite Lita Bane's suite. He grinned. He made a vague gesture with his big hand.

"Come in and have a drink, Maroni," said the man in the doorway, holding out a bottle. Maroni decided suddenly that he needed another drink. Somewhere in the back of his mind lingered the thought that he had done something tonight he shouldn't have done. Talked? Argued? Sang? Whatever it was, a drink would help. He mumbled, wobbled across the heavily-carpeted passageway. The man in the doorway, smiling, stepped aside. Maroni stumbled in. The door swung shut behind him. The man with the bottle said, "Take off your hat, Maroni." There was a peculiar look in his eyes, a flat deadliness in his voice. He seemed to be looking past Maroni. His empty hand shot out, knocked the black fedora from the big man's head.

"Why — you — you — " mumbled Maroni, blazing to anger. But he didn't get to name the man for what he was.

Another man had been behind the door, another man who bore in his hands a gleaming noose of silvered piano wire. He stepped forward. The wire noose flashed through the air. Maroni jerked backward. The gadget slid tight about his bull-like neck. He turned, gagging, and in desperation struck at the man who had placed the instrument of death about his neck! But the blow stopped midway, as if the wrist had hung upon an invisible hook. A look of pained amazement overspread his battered features. His eyes began to protrude. His great mouth was open for a hoarse yell that did not, could not, issue. The first man raised the whiskey bottle and brought it down sharply on Maroni's head.

In her boudoir, the woman who had been Lita Bane, had disappeared. Before her mirror she had removed the small strips of flesh colored plaster that pulled the outer corners of her eyes upward. A handful of grease had removed the white sheen from her features, revealing the healthy brownness of her real skin. Quickly she fluffed her hair about her face, parted it on

the side. Tissue removed the heavy red of lipstick from her lips. She stepped out of the lounging pajamas, thrust long silken legs into a hotel chambermaid uniform. The silken hose were pealed off, cheap service-weights took their place. A plain blue coat, a flat, unattractive hat.

She observed herself in the mirror, went into the bathroom and emerged with a pair of towels hanging over her arm. For a moment she stood in the center of the room, biting her lip in thought. Then, throwing back her shoulders resolutely, she walked to the door.

Opening it, stepping into the passageway, she noted that the door to he suite across the hall was slowly opening. Quickly she turned around to her own suite, said in a high pitched voice—"Goodnight, Miz Bane, and I hopes ye rest well, and I thank ye again for the money, I do."

She closed the door firmly, content that she heard the lock click into place, turned and shuffled down the hallway toward the service elevator.

Afterward she came to know that had she looked over her shoulder she might have seen the white, twisted face of death peering after her from the suite across the hall.

CHAPTER IX

Cards on the Table

DOCTOR THADDEUS HARKER had a theory concerning weeping women. In his younger days he tried various ways to console them; experience taught him in later years there was but one thing to do—to let them weep, cry it out. Consequently, he sat silently wrapped in thought on his side of the red coupe, the woman, Jeannie Wright—or Jeannie Zachary —occupying the middle.

Hercules Jones, however, had not arrived at the age of wisdom. Sight and sound of a woman, particularly an attractive woman, in tears, saddened him. He drove with misty eyes. Clumsily he laid a hand on Jeannie Wright's shoulder, said, "Lookit, now ma'am, crying ain't going to help it a bit!"

She raised her head, glared at him, shook his hand from her shoulders. "You," she gasped, "you! How do I know it wasn't you? What have you done with him, what were you prowling around for, what have you done with Shag?"

"Who, me?" Aggrievedly Hercules swung the red car around a lumbering truck. "Look lady, I ain't never seen no guy named Shag Zachary. Heck, me and doc is just trying to help you out."

Doc Harker chuckled. "Indeed, my dear, Hercules is right. Believe me, I had only your interest at heart when I took you out of the Southern Club a few minutes ago. Mister—ah—Melton seems to have been quite wrought up, and also your spotless, lilywhite chief of police, Mr. Thames. You, too, were angry and when angry people get together—" He snapped his fingers. "Spontaneous combustion."

She looked at him oddly. "Maybe," she agreed, "I should thank you at that. And on the other hand maybe you're not all you pretend to be."

"Maybe," acquiesced the doctor. "Maybe Georgie, your *brother,* has been talking."

Sullenly she said, "Georgie isn't my brother. He used to—well—he claims to be a friend of Shag's." She closed her lips, grimly, her jaw set—as if determined not to say more. The car sped on through the night. For the first

time, she seemed to realize where she was being taken. Her fingers found Herk's big arm, her anxious voice said, "Hey, after what happened back there you can't go to Resthaven! Melton and Thames and the others will—"

"Exactly," said the doctor, a bit sharply. "And what if they do? You forget, Miss Zachary, that there are some twenty five thousand souls in this town, and not all of them are crooked. Melton—or Thames—or any of the others might do almost anything on their own stamping grounds. I doubt very much whether they will risk coming after us once we are—you might say in the open."

He remained quiet for a few seconds, allowing the angry, frightened woman to realize the wisdom of his statement, to draw what comfort and consolation from it that she could. Presently, her hysteria seemed to die away; somehow or other, she retained a grip on herself, and by the time they wheeled into the gravel drive of Resthaven Courts she was sitting stiff and erect, staring out through the steamy windshield in sullen silence. She did not even protest when they rolled past the office and down the drive to Number 34.

Doctor Thaddeus Harker switched on the light. The first glance from his suspicious eyes showed that the cabin was exactly as they had left it, no one had bothered their accoutrements again. He turned, "Ma'am," he said in his gentle voice, "to such as we have, you are more than welcome. May I invite you to partake of a spot of bourbon whiskey?" He poured two drinks, one of which she took. The door opened and Hercules entered, his tommy-gun clutched tightly to his huge breast. His face beamed like that of a child with a new toy.

Doctor Harker said, "Hercules,

please stay outside, and keep watch, just in case. Miss Zachary and I wish to talk of many things."

Hercules looked disappointed. "But lookit, doc.—"

"You can take it apart tomorrow, to see what makes it go," reassured the little doctor. Hercules laid the gun carefully on a bed and went out, slamming the door behind him. Doctor Harker raised his glass. His eyes were bright and wary, like those of a bird. "Shall we drink," he said, and, as she raised her glass, "to nine hundred thousand dollars worth of bonds?"

THE woman looked puzzled, turned the toast over and over in her mind and finally shrugged, slightly, before drinking.

The doctor wiped his moustaches carefully. "My dear," he beamed, "you have been a great disappointment to me, after a fashion." He raised his hand as she started to protest, apologized profusely. "I simply meant, my dear, that I rather pride myself on reading character. After my talk with you at the office, I was quite content with all the information you gave out, and I must say you are a consummate actress."

She sniffed accusingly, her voice was cold. "As soon as I found out you were trying to pump me I decided to fill you to the brim with misinformation. What's the difference? Now suppose you tell me who you are and why you were being held by Luke Melton and why you bought me back out here."

Doctor Harker bowed. He opened the portmanteau, extracted a great loose leaf scrapbook. "Ma'am," he said courteously, "you will find here hundreds of letters from all parts of the country rendering thanks to me from sufferers, who have found the efficacy

and efficiency of *Chickasha Remedies* exactly as I have described. I am, in short, a medicine man, old style, who goes from town to town relieving pain, aiding the sick, and incidentally making a living."

"And I suppose Melton and Thames were trying to make you come through with a few packages, or bottles, of the stuff for nothing?" Harker decided she was beautiful, even when she sneered like she did now.

"Suppose," he said, twisting his moustache, "that we—ah—lay the cards on the table. I will be utterly frank with you. For years, my dear, I have been fascinated by crime and criminals. I have, in my poor way, been able through some small ability that I might possess, to solve several crimes in several cities. I am like the hound that has sucked an egg—after the first, there was no stopping me. Now, I shall put myself entirely in your hands. I came here to help solve a crime, or rather, to help clear up a bad condition. Oddly enough, as soon as I arrive I find that the condition is practically cleared up. Which leaves me at loose ends, so to speak."

She shifted uneasily in the chair, glanced at her wrist watch. "And enables me," he said softly, "to turn my services and abilities, such as they are, to you."

"You mean," she said suspiciously, "you're a sort of a private detective and you want to work for me? What could you do for me?"

"Possibly," he said soothingly, "I could find out something about Shag Zachary for you. It may be that I even know something about him now."

At mention of her brother's name she leaped to her feet, would have gone through the door, except for his restraining hand. For a moment it looked as though she meant to claw his eyes out, then, like a tired and distracted child she began crying, against the wide lapel of the Prince Albert coat. Bit by bit the thing came out.

"You've simply got to understand that Shag isn't bad," she told him. "Shag got off on the wrong foot. He was smarter than most young fellows, and once he was in it, once he knew there was no backing out, he decided to make the best of it, to make it pay him. He did! But Shag wasn't really bad!"

Quickly she ran over a few of Shag's exploits, how he stayed always in the background; how, to most people, Shag Zachary was merely a name; but how in reality he pulled the strings that made the puppets dance. And pay. At last the G-heat had gotten on him, and they had stuck him for several things, including income tax evasion. And the rumor had grown and grown, while he was in prison, that Shag Zachary was broke.

"And of course," prompted Doctor Harker, "Shag wasn't broke?"

She shook her head. "He wanted everyone to think he was. Shag had only one idea, that was to get out of the rackets. Even after eleven years in stir you know it would be hard for him to quit. So he wanted to arrange it to get out of the country."

"How long have you had this place, Miss Zachary?"

"Four years. Shag gave me the money to buy it with." She looked at him defiantly. "And I've run it fair and square, Doctor Harker. No matter what you might think, I've kept it clean. The rest of the town—" She shrugged.

"The rest of the town," he said softly, "has giving shelter to criminals. But you haven't. Why?"

"BECAUSE I wanted the place to get and keep a good name. I wasn't sure what plans Shag had. I thought perhaps when he got out he'd have to stay somewhere a few months before he could get loose ends together. It wouldn't look so fine for him to live at a tourist camp with a shady reputation."

He nodded sagely. "And Shag was released three days ago. He headed right for here?"

It was her turn to nod. Now her jaw muscles tightened again, gleamed white. "Right for here, alone."

"And why did you go to Melton?" She shook her head stubbornly. "I'll talk, my dear, and you tell me if I'm right." He sat down, crossed his thin knees, careful of his creases. He drew a black stogie from his pocket, gazed at it sorrowfully, thrust it back, deciding not to offend the lady. She sat with her hands clasped tightly in her lap.

"Let us assume," he said gently, "that your brother, Shag, possessed a cache, perhaps a safe deposit box, that was never uncovered by the Federals. Let us assume that your brother spent his time in prison adding to the rumor that he was broke, that he did all possible to foster this rumor. His plans, as you have admitted, were to leave the country, and, I assume, to take you with him."

"Of course," she said stiffly.

He made a church steeple of his fingers. "This, naturally, is mere assumption, my dear. Prison grapevine in days like these is fairly complete and accurate. Suppose that through deft inquiry, and he had plenty of time for inquiry, he learned of Abbottsville. Suppose he learned that a group of men practically had the town in their hands, men who were oblivious to the presence of criminals, as long as those criminals paid a high price for immunity. It followed then, that somewhere in the town of Abbottsville was a safe—ah—fence.

"It looked like an ideal spot to Shag Zachary. He advanced the money for you, his sister, to go into business in Abbottsville, several years ago. Shag was known for his shrewdness, t i m e meant nothing to him. Surely at the end of four years, careful inquiry would show you whom to approach."

"Approach?" s h e asked. "You're simply guessing. I d o n ' t know what y o u ' r e talking about."

He beamed at her, held up an admonitory finger. "Now, now! You approached the proper men. You told them that upon Shag's release he would be in town with a large gob of securities and bonds, which he wished to sell."

"You ought to know," she snapped, "that Shag has learned his lesson. Why should he fence bonds that aren't hot? Would he plant hot stuff in his cache, a man as shrewd as my brother?"

"We're getting no place," the doctor was a bit provoked. It all fell in so beautifully. In his mind's eye he was picturing the man with the yellow gloves, who had been blasted off the road by the sedan. The man whom Herk Jones claimed to have found dead in the garage, a wire garrotte about his neck. "The reason is very plain. He has already been stuck for income tax evasion. He wants more than anything else to get out of the country—with money. Cash money, we'll say. Should he take the bonds—which may not be hot at all—to a regular broker, the

government will be on his neck again. Now, my dear, just how much did your brother have in his cache?" Silence. "Could it have been nine hundred thousand dollars?"

Doctor Harker knew it was a large sum, not only from Luke Melton's statement but from what had occurred. The fact that the ring in Abbottsville had cleaned the town of the shady element— doubtless at S h a g Zachary's insistence— proved the money to be of importance and size, as to amount.

She n o d d e d her head. "It might have been," she said shortly, "It was, at least, big enough to make them——" Suddenly she began to sob, her head came down on her hands, her slim shoulders trembled. "What have they done with him? Where is he? All he asked was to be let alone. He was through with crime; all he wanted was to get away—!"

Doctor Thaddeus Clay Harker moved toward the bourbon bottle. He poured one drink, looked at Jeannie Zachary, then poured a drink for her.

> To whom it may concern:
>
> Dr. Harker's treatment was terrific. I am now enjoying my sudden vacation from Abbottsville.
>
> (signed) Luke Melton

OUTSIDE Hercules Jones, still dinner-jacket clad, hunched his shoulders against the rawness of the late breeze and paced from one shadow to another. Herk didn't think of the dead man he had found, the disappearing corpse; rather he thought of Brenda Sloan. He thought of the tough-faced monkey who had been with Brenda at the Abbott House, wished mightily that he had heaved him into the fountain. Getting tough! The louse! And being with Brenda! He veered to thoughts of the tommy-gun laying on the bed inside the house and wished that the doctor would hurry up with his palaver so he, Hercules, could take the thing apart and see what made it go.

The headlights of a car pulled off the highway and into the court. A horn blew. The negro porter came out of the office and hopped on the side of the car. In a moment he went back into the office, emerged again and resumed his stance. Herk stepped into the shelter of a porch column as the car headed down the drive.

Four cabins away it stopped. The porter got off, opened the door of the cottage, switched on the light. The driver of the car backed it into the shelter, rather than headed it in. Doctor Harker might have made something of this—perhaps the person was fixing to leave quickly if occasion demanded. Hercules Jones didn't. He watched a woman in a plain blue coat and shapeless hat get out and thought nothing of it. Presently the nego porter went slouching up the drive toward the office. Herk continued his restless pacing.

Minutes passed. His thoughts went from Brenda to the tommy-gun and back to Brenda. He didn't see a thing —he heard it. The soft crunch of gravel beneath a foot. Quickly he pulled the lapels of his coat together, to cover the whiteness of his shirt bosom. Now he made out a stooped figure, keeping well toward the cottages, approaching on cautious feet. He grinned to himself, flexed his muscles. Sneaking up, hanh? Like that, hanh?

Almost he could have touched the moving shadow as it glided past him. It stooped, peered into the crack of light left by the short window shade. Hercules grinned like an ape, drew back his foot, and swung it. The fig-ure flew through the air, landed on its hands and knees. Hercules grasped it by the shoulders, jerked it to its feet, hissed. "Spying around are you, Georgie! Damn you, I'll—" Words died away to a rumble in his thick chest. He managed, "Brenda! Brenda! Aw gee—I'm—I'm—Brenda"

"You big oaf," she grated, "I'll never be able to walk again. Get me in the house, let me see what's been broken!"

He had her in his arms now, patting her, making over her like a mother over a hurt child. "We can't go in the house, honey. Doc's got a dame in there!" And when she stiffened in his arms, "Not what you think. It's a dame named Zachary. She's Shag Zachary's sister."

Brenda groaned. "Gosh Almighty, let's get in the trailer, then. Any place!"

They moved toward the bulk of the red safe-on-wheels, Brenda limping in the lead. Hercules whispered hoarsely, "Hey, we can't go in there. I ain't got my keys."

"Go in the house and get them then," she commanded. "The woman has seen you, she knows you're around. I tell you I've got a broken—ah—well, anyway I want in that trailer."

Obediently Herk started for the front door. She heard him tap. Still wincing in pain, she reached up toward the knob that opened the safe-on-wheels. To her surprise the knob twisted in her fingers. The door was open.

She stepped up into the trailer, fumbled for the light switch. The trailer flooded with light. But only for a moment. She stood aghast staring down at the thing on the floor. She flipped off the light and stepped outside the trailer, closing the door and leaning against it, her eyes wide with amazement, her bosom rising and falling with excitement, her hurts forgotten.

The thing on the floor was a dead man. Staring down at him, his bulging eyeballs had appeared to be glaring directly up at her. His two hands were grotesquely twisted over his stomach and chest, like a boxer ready to defend himself. The gloves covering the hand were brilliant yellow in color.

CHAPTER X

Discourteous Dr. Harker

DOCTOR THADDEUS HARKER put the picture Jeannie Zachary had brought to him—a picture of her brother—carefully in his pocket and regarded Brenda Sloan and Hercules Jones with unbelieving eyes. Doctor Harker prided himself on his poker face, but now he found it difficult to keep his goatee from quivering with excitement. "A corpse," he said, fighting to keep his voice calm, "in the trailer? Ridiculous!" And then he remembered that when Hercules had been slugged, earlier in the evening, his pockets had been turned inside out, his key to the trailer had been taken among others. Stiffly he said, "Stay here," and went out into the night. A few seconds later he was kneeling beside the dead man, who had called himself Stanley. The rays of a small flashlight illuminated the strained, blackened face, and the photograph in the doctor's hand, the photograph of Shag Zachary, who had been on his way to Abbottsville when disaster met him.

He grunted, flipped out his light, went back in the house and reached for the bourbon bottle. Brenda and Hercules watched him with anxious eyes. Downing his liquor neat he shrugged.

"Never mind the nervousness! I suppose you are both wondering just what this is all about. We'll disregard the dead man momentarily. Now listen to what I have learned, Brenda, and tell me, in turn, how it checks with what you have found out. All of which, undoubtedly, will lead us back to the corpse of—ah—Mr. Stanley!"

Carefully he enumerated the points of the affair. How Wallace had written him, asking his help in cleaning up Abbottsville, the town he loved, how he had talked to Wallace on the phone and Wallace had asserted that the town had cleaned itself up!

Brenda nodded. She said, "It's odd, but it's a fact. Both Carson Thames and Luigi Maroni told me practically the same thing. There must be some reason—"

"There is," said the doctor dryly. "Nine hundred thousand dollars worth of reason. We have, according to all I can learn, five men practically controlling the town, Thames, Carter, Chambers, Melton and Maroni. These men had a nice thing in Abbottsville. Unless there was hope of doing better, they would hardly have changed the layout."

He went on to tell Brenda, in a matter of fact voice that Shag Zachary, ex-racketeer, was the hope of doing better. That Shag Zachary had arranged, through his sister, to cash in on the contents of his remaining cache through the Abbottsville gang.

Brenda said slowly, "That seems to agree with what Maroni told me just tonight. With this exception — he seemed to think that because he had, in the old days, been a pal of Zachary's, Zachary would do business only with him."

Doctor Harker once more poured bourbon in his glass. He peered at the brown liquor. "Mmmmmm. I think we will kill a couple of birds with one stone, children. Now listen closely. Here is what I want you to do. How you do it, I don't care. But do it. You will go into town, the pair of you, and you, Brenda, because Hercules is so big, will rent a drive-it-yourself car. You will bring five gallons of kerosene. You will also obtain approximately two pounds of dry ice—if you have to steal it. And you will get back here as soon as possible. Perhaps you can compare notes on the way, and thus save me a lot of explanations."

As they left, Doctor Harker turned out the lights of the cottage. He hoped they would return in ample time. He waited fully ten minutes before going back to the red trailer that was a safe on wheels. Working swifly in the darkness, he carried several instruments, some of them quite bulky, into the cabin. He crawled beneath the trailer with a screw driver, worked swiftly and silently, dragging the huge box he detached also into the cabin. His last trip brought in the dead man's body. Again he worked in darkness.

At fifteen minutes after one, Hercules and Brenda were back, unquestioning. What was the use to question a sphinx? The huge box that the doctor had detached from the trailer sat in one corner of the cabin. To all appearances, lid removed, it seemed filled with storage batteries. Hercules knew the box was a fake, knew it contained two real batteries only. The others were merely faked tops! He lifted the end one, thrust half the dry ice down beneath it, lifted that on the opposite end and did the same with the resultant half. Over the whole he spread a blanket. The box was shoved beneath the bed in the front room.

Hercules choked. He gazed with horror at the bed, looked dumbly at the man who directed his destinies. Never, in his memory, had the little doctor treated a man, dead or alive, so discourteously. Doctor Harker shrugged. "Come on," he said a bit grimly, "and listen closely." Wordlessly, as usual, they came.

AT THIRTY minutes past one o'clock, the town of Abbottsville was treated to an unusual sight. A red coupe having a red, oblong trailer attached to it, careened through the main street of town. It's horn pressed down, as if it had stuck, blared painfully like a beast in torment! Very plainly could be seen the muzzle of a shotgun protruding from a slot in the rear, and from time to time that shotgun roared, filled the night with its red horror. Nor was that all! Half a block behind the speeding fortress on wheels came a black sedan, the muzzle of a tommygun thrust through the broken windshield. An orange cone of flame seemed attached to the muzzle as the man behind it held his finger tightly on the trigger.

The two cars and the trailer shot through the town at great speed. So swiftly had they materialized out of nowhere that they were gone before startled police commandeered cars to pursue. Luke Melton saw the trailer from the upper wind of the Southern Club. Amos Carter, the newspaper editor and publisher, saw them sweep past his home in a swirl of bullets. Honest John Chambers, the mayor, peered fearfully from his upper window to see the battle on wheels, and Thames, the chief of police, cursed at Melton's elbow in the Southern Club.

Only Maroni failed to see the pyrotechnics. Maroni was dead in a suite at the Abbott House.

By the time Carson Thames came up to the trailer where it lay, overturned in a vacant lot, it was a mass of flaming, molten metal and fittings. A crowd of people was about it, a motorcycle policeman and a beat walker were talking to Doctor Harker and Hercules Jones, who stood watching the ruin ruefully.

Harker was trembling, actually blubbering with fear, saying, "And suddenly, for no reason at all that I can see, persons began to shoot at us from the underbrush. It seemed like there were three of them but I couldn't very well distinguish their features. I was working in the trailer—with my assistant—and we fired back at them.

"My assistant managed to get out of the trailer and into our car. We decided we'd be safer in town, but, as you saw, it was not so. We may have gotten two of the men who fired at us, because I think only one was in the sedan that followed us into town. I carried quite a few chemicals in the trailer, and one of the bullets must have set them off. Hercules, my assistant, turned the corner here and you can see what happened." He gazed about fearfully, laid a hand on Herk's big arm.

"Lookit," said Hercules meaningly to the police, "the sedan went that away."

Thames, listening beside Melton, took charge. He said, "Suppose we go down to the station, Doctor Harker, and get all the details. We certainly can't have such things happening in our town! I see you managed to get your car unhooked. One of the boys will ride down with your man, you can go down with Melton and I."

"All right," quivered Harker. "You gentlemen are more than considerate, I assure you. Hercules, the gentleman in uniform will ride back downtown with you."

As he took his place in the rear seat of Thames' big car, he looked over at the remains of the gutted trailer. It still glowed red hot. No one could poke about it for some time. A brief, sly smile of satisfaction lit his face, only to vanish instantly as Melton, the gambler, turned to him.

Melton said, "Nice going, Doctor, nice going."

BRENDA SLOAN left the Drive-It-Yourself with the broken windshield in an alley. She left the tommygun on the seat, thinking somehow that its abandonment would break Herk's heart. At least, she thought, as she stole away from the car, Herk had had the fun of firing it at the trailer for a while! For it had been Hercules driving the rented car as they careened through Abbottsville. Only when they paused at the vacant lot had they traded seats and jobs, as Doc Harker touched the match to the kerosene soaked trailer.

Fortunately she was able to enter the hotel unobserved, to ride up to her floor in the automatic service elevator and enter her own suite. It was a matter of moments to resume her former status of Lita Bane. And only a few more moments until she laid, pajama clad, on her own bed and turned the events of the night over and over in her shrewd mind. Hercules had told her of the original meeting with Stanley, of finding of the corpse, the blow on his own head. Doctor Harker had told her of Zachary. And Brenda Sloan, after putting two and two together, was immensely sorry for Jeannie Zachary.

To her, the dead man, who had evidently burned in the trailer, was Shag Zachary. She shuddered a bit there on her bed, for she could not reconcile the doctor's character with the disposal of that corpse!

Afterward she remembered that it was nearly two-thirty when the knock came on her door. There were policemen there, detectives and men in uniform. Policemen, and the chief of police, Carson Thames, as well as the medical examiner, Rudolph Blitz. Yes, she said readily, she had been with Maroni that night. He had left her around eleven, she believed. No, she didn't know where he had gone, home presumably.

When she saw the corpse of the man who had loved her, she might have fainted, had not Carson Thames caught her. Maroni looked horrible.

AT THE police station, Herk Jones listened open mouthed to his boss. He knew Doctor Harker for a consummate actor, yet the little doctor surpassed his best.

"I tell you," he babbled, saliva white on his lips, "that I want protection! Someone or somebody in this town is out for me. I can't possibly leave until tomorrow, and they'll kill me in the meantime! You've got to protect me the rest of the night."

He blubbered, he actually cried, he was the picture of abject fear. Luke Melton shrugged and turned away. Hercules was ashamed of the doctor, he turned red and shifted uneasily from one foot to the other. Carson Thames said with curled lips, "What do you expect me to do?" The look he gave Melton said plainly, "And to think we suspected this snivelling old goat of having guts!"

Doctor Thaddeus Harker was indeed a pitiful sight. His clothes were awry, his eyes rolled, his moustaches were bedraggled. He looked wildly to-

ward the door, toward the window, piteously back to Thames. "Let me sleep in jail!" he babbled. "In jail, where there'll be iron bars about me, protection at least, where no one can get at me! Please, please."

And when Hercules Jones went disconsolately out into the night, his employer and idol was safely behind the bars of the Abbottsville jail, though why he should want to be imprisoned was more than Herk could see. Nor why he, Hercules, was to do what he had been instructed to do!

He made one stop, at the telegraph station. He sent a wire, as per instructions, to one Howard Smith, in Little Rock, telling him that he wanted three or four cases of *Chickasha Remedies* air expressed to Abbottsville at once. He signed the doctor's name to the order.

He drove out the highway they had traversed on entering Abbottsville, after making certain that he was not followed. He glanced at an envelope where Doctor Harker had inscribed some figures. When the speedometer of the red coupe reached the figure on the envelope he stopped the car. Alighting he found, to his surprise, that he was practically in the same spot where the coupe of Stanley, the corpse, had run back on the road! There was the culvert—and there were the deep tire marks. Grunting his disdain he walked across to where the dead man's coupe had parked, stopped quickly. His great fingers swept up several handfuls of the gritty dirt, dropped it in a manila envelope. He went back to the car wondering just why he was picking up dirt on a foggy, rainy night, miles from Abbottsville.

Back at Resthaven he stole quietly down to the garage where he had seen the dead man, repeated the same maneuver. On that envelope, he wrote with his pencil stub, *Garage Resthaven*.

Back in Number 34 he changed his clothes, donned a dark shirt, put a heavy pair of wool socks in his pockets, found a jimmy and picklock in the apparatus from the burned trailer. He went out the back door of the cabin and walked across a cornfield toward town, muttering to himself.

"An' if I get caught," he said bitterly, "this bunch of jayhawks will throw the book at me. I wish I knew what the devil this was all about."

* * *

Doctor Thaddeus Harker spent a sleepless night. Not that he was frightened, only that he was fastidious, and jails annoyed him. He sat primly on the edge of a cot smoking stogie after stogie, reasoning with his shrewd little mind. Hunch had sent him to this jail, hunch pure and simple. He had worked on the farmer's "lost mule" theory. The farmer, so successful at finding wandering animals, who, upon being questioned as to his success, answered simply, "Well, I just put myself in a mule's place, and go where I figure I'd go if I was a mule. And there's the mule."

Where he asked himself, would a man in fear of his life, hide out? The answer, to him, was jail, considering everything.

Around three o'clock he was aroused by a visitor.

The visitor was Doctor Rudolph Blitz. Blitz' eyes shone with excitement. He seemed beside himself. "I thought I ought to get you up," he babbled. "Something terrible has happened. My uncle, Arthur Wallace—he's dead! I just found him at home in bed, with a wire contraption around his throat, garrotted."

CHAPTER XI

A Deal Is Made

*T*HE Abbottsville jail could hardly be called the *ne plus ultra* of penal institutions. It was old. It was dirty and rusty from disuse. It had a musty, dusty office, but no jailer to occupy it. Seldom had it sheltered a prisoner, other than a drunk, in the past few years. When the first dirty streaks of dawn streamed through the barred window, Doctor Thaddeus Harker arose. He found the door of his cell ajar, found that it opened into the dusty bullpen. Up and down this bullpen he paced, his hands behind his back, his head bowed in thought.

Stanley, the supposed cosmetic salesman, dead with a wire garotte about his thoat! Wallace, the man who had summoned him to Abbottsville, dead in the same manner. He recalled his phone call the night before, his doubt as to the identity of the man who answered and talked so hoarsely, claiming to be Wallace. The mention of scotch whiskey, the name Thad, rather than Warsaw. Could it be, he wondered, that he had talked to the actual killer? And what kind of killer would have nerve enough to answer the phone when his victim lay dead beside him?

Back and forth he paced, the smoke from his foul stogie streaming behind him like blue plumes. Doctor Thaddeus Harker was on his mettle now. Before, he simply had been anxious to earn the fee mentioned by Arthur Wallace for cleaning out a crime nest. Now his friend and client had been taken away from him, he was doubly resolved to carry out his original purpose. He owed it to Wallace!

A man emerged from an opposite

cell, nodded briefly at the doctor and went to the lavatory at the end of the bullpen. He washed his face and hands, dried them on a dirty handkerchief and went back to his cell in his sock feet. The doctor continued to pace the floor. Presently, from the opposite cell came the sound of heavy breathing, almost a snore. Softly Harker crossed the foul floor, stood looking at the man. A two days growth of beard obscured his features. He wore no tie, his shirt collar was up about his throat. His clothes were bedraggled, yet damp and mud splattered. His shoes sat at the end of the barred shelf that served as a cot.

Softly Doc Harker entered the cell. By the dim light he studied the face. It might—or it might not be, he concluded. Very cautiously, he reached for the shoes. Once outside the cell, back in his own cubicle, he spread an old letter on the floor. His pearl handled knife scraped mud and debris from the shoes, from the sole, the heel, the welt itself. He folded the letter carefully so the accumulation of dirt would not spill, put it in an envelope, wrote across the envelope, "Bum in Jail." He returned the shoes to their owner, pausing just long enough to gaze again in rapt contemplation at the sleeper.

Doctor Thaddeus Harker, in his younger days, had done the come-on act for his own medicine show. He was an escape artist. From the sweatband on his white hat he took various pieces of spring steel. From the cuff of his trousers he extracted a stiffer piece of metal, curiously shaped, three minutes later he opened the door of the bullpen and stepped to the corridor. There was no one in the dingy office. In the second drawer of the littered desk he found the rusty master key that opened all cells as well as the bullpen.

Out in the street he walked three blocks, went into a cafe, drank a cup of coffee, called a cab and set out for Resthaven, well satisfied with his night's work. The Harker luck had held up.

HERCULES JONES lay flat on his back in the bed, his mouth open, a raucous noise issuing from between those thick and battered lips. He sat up sleepily, rubbed his eyes, said, "Lookit, doc, why don't you open up? I got to know what you're doing or I quit, see? This shooting around in the dark won't—"

"Did you get them?" asked the doctor briefly. Herk subsided, pointed at the bureau. There, in a neat row, reposed six left shoes, each one labelled with a shipping tag. Moodily Hercules said, "I did all the damn crazy things you said to do, doc. And it damned near got me killed. That newspaper guy, that Carter, not only had a pair of police dogs but he had a shotgun, too, a shotgun he wasn't afraid to use!"

But Doc Harker paid him no attention. He jerked off his Prince Albert, dragged a chemist's smock from his portmanteau, donned it. He picked up the first shoe, tagged *Georgie Vasey,* scraped mud and debris from it exactly as he had done to the bum's shoe in the jail where he had spent the night!

Over his shoulder he said, "I'm going to be very busy for most of the day, Hercules. Dress, eat breakfast, go to town. Find out all the details concerning the death of Arthur Wallace. I want particularly to know what time he died, if it's been established. Find out on what charge the bum in the jail was arrested—and when. Call Lita Bane, at the Abbott house, and tell her this."

Open-mouthed, Hercules Jones listened. When he had finished, he said, "Dead men all around us a-raising hell and putting a chunk under it! And you want to have a party. You slay me, doc, you slay me."

When he was fully dressed and leaving, he turned at the door. Gloomily he said, "You know that big monkey Brenda was with at dinner?"

Doctor Harker grunted, went on with his scraping.

"Never," said Hercules in disgust, "am I going to have a chance to twist his fat neck. About three this morning Brenda called me to the office phone. The guy went and got hisself killed, right across the hall from Brenda, with a wire gadget around his neck just like the little guy Stanley had!"

The doctor stared down at the shoe he was scraping so meticulously. Softly as if to himself, he said, "Stanley! Maroni! Wallace! I begin to see a pattern." The door closed, the doctor continued to stare at the shoe in his hand. The door opened. Hercules said, "Brenda thought you might like to know, but I told her you was in jail."

Hercules entered the red coupe and started on his errands. His not to reason why, his but to do and die! For something about which he knew nothing!

SHORTLY after nine o'clock the doctor answered the door to admit Jeannie Wright—Zachary. She wore a blue wool, slack suit with a wide leather belt that accented the smooth flare of her hips. She sank down in a chair and glared at the doctor, who, at her knock, had quickly tossed a sheet over the table and dresser where he had been working.

She said, "You've heard what happened in town, haven't you?"

He nodded gravely. "Maroni—and Arthur Wallace. Garrotted." He didn't mention Stanley—nor did she.

Her voice grew husky, her eyes narrowed. "And I just received a telephone call telling me that I'd get the same unless I pulled up stakes and left here before noon. What do you make of that, if you're a detective?"

"Why," he said mildly, "I'm sure it all fits together somewhere, some way, and I'm sure it all has something to do with your brother."

Miserably, she nodded. Her voice was a dull chant as she lost control of herself. "All he wants is a chance, just a chance to get out of the country with a little money, that's all. He isn't bad, he doesn't want to go back into the rackets! Do you know what I think?"

He waited, brows lifted.

"I think my brother is dead!"

After a while the doctor said softly, "Suppose I assure you that your brother is not dead, ma'am? Now listen to me. If I were to get you and your brother safely out of this—and if he isn't dead, you can rest assured he is in as much danger as you are—I say, *if* I get you safely out of this, could you persuade your brother to make peace with the feds, to pay what he should pay out of the bonds he brought in? To make a deal, we'll say?"

She considered this for a long time. "The bonds he has, and the securities," she admitted, "aren't hot. Shag was too smart for that. It's just this: He's stubborn and hard-headed. The government took a big fine from him, and eleven years of his life. He feels that's enough. Now, if he markets his securities openly—they'll take a big spot of them, maybe tie them up legally."

"Which," said the doctor dryly, "is much better than being killed for the full amount. Half a loaf—you know.

Suppose you answer my question. Could you persuade your brother to make a deal?"

"I think I could," she said shortly, "if he thought my life was in danger otherwise."

"And I can assure you that it is, my dear." He rummaged in the portmanteau again, came out with a short, snub-nosed pistol. "You are now a client of mine, and intensely valuable to me. I want you to keep this with you, constantly. And do not be afraid to use it should occasion demand. And do not forget our agreement."

She took the gun, looked at him with narrowed eyes. "So I'm your client," she mused. "You're going to dig my brother and his securities out of your hat and for that, I'll owe you what?"

He bowed magnanimously. "My fees are usually left up to the beneficiaries of my endeavors," he said softly. "The only thing I really expect from you is the fulfillment of your promise. That your brother—if and when I find him —will make a deal with the federal men."

She nodded her head, thrust out her hand. The doctor's white fingers closed over it.

Someone rapped at the door. The doctor opened it. Georgie Vasey stood with his eyes on the doctor's stomach. He said, "Phone call for my sister."

And before either of them could answer he turned on his heel and went back down the drive toward the office. Jeannie thrust the gun into a pocket, followed him. Doctor Harker closed the door, went back to his instruments.

AROUND noon Hercules returned. Moodily he made his report. Arthur Wallace had been killed around eight forty-five. The time was practically positive, arrived at by none other

than Carson Thames himself. Wallace had been garrotted, as Blitz had said, and in threshing about, had knocked a clock from the table, breaking it, stopping it at exactly fifteen minutes before nine.

Doctor Harker took this information gravely. To himself he said: *At eight fifty I talked to Wallace—apparently.* And he knew then that his suspicions had been correct, that the voice that had spoken to him over the phone was not that of his old friend, Arthur Wallace! That Wallace had already threshed his life out on the floor at the time of the call. Why? Why? Why? The question drummed itself over and over in his silver thatched head. First Stanley! Then Maroni! And now Wallace!

"Who found the corpse?"

"A guy named Blitz. You know him, Wallace's son-in-law. Found it about two, or three, in the morning. The daughter is out of town, visiting. There wasn't any servants, just Blitz and Wallace living alone. Blitz has an alibi all right, if that's what you're thinking."

Doc Harker shook his head, poured himself a drink.

"The bum," said Hercules, "was arrested around seven, for busting the window of a liquor store." He peered at the doctor. There was no sign on the benign features that this meant anything. Reluctantly he went on, "Brenda says she'll have the party all right, and she'll have the people there you told her to have."

Still no answer. The doctor swirled the liquor around in his glass. Stanley, Maroni and Wallace! The three of them! Why? Why? Why?

"Lookit doc," said Hercules desperately, "if Wallace was your customer, how do you expect to make anything out of this with him dead? What's the idea of all these goings on now? What are we going to do?"

Doctor Harker said, "I'm very busy, Hercules. But if it will set your puzzled mind at ease, I'm going to produce a triple murderer, I'm going to run the head rats out of the city of Abbottsville. I'm going to find a missing man— a living corpse—and I'm going to aid and assist t h e United S t a t e s Government at the same time. Now will you leave me alone? Go some place, do anything, only be back here by six o'clock tonight."

Hercules closed the door behind him glumly.

> **To who wants to know:**
>
> **The only trouble with Dr. Harker is he keeps his stuff too much to himself —but he is a right guy, anyhow, and his treatments is okay, too.**
>
> **(signed) Hercules Jones**

CHAPTER XII

A Line-up of—Shoes

SHE was breathlessly lovely that night, even more so than she had ever appeared to those men who had known and admired her for the past month. The light danced down from overhead and gleamed lovingly on the sleek blackness of her hair. Again she wore a white evening gown, backless, extreme, moulded to her lush curves like wet tissue paper.

The party was in the Blue Room of the Abbott House, and if any of the guests were uneasy at the strangeness of the waiters—evidently new to the hostelry—they were too entertained to comment. For the banquet was sumptuous.

Brenda Sloan, alias Lita Bane, arose from her chair at the head of the table.

She looked down its gleaming expanse at her guests, Carson Thames, Honest John Chambers, Amos Carter, Luke Melton, Rudolph Blitz. At the end of the table was an empty chair.

"Friends," she said in that throaty voice of hers, "perhaps you have wondered why I wanted you all to dine with me tonight of all nights." She paused for a moment, swept the upturned faces with her own oriental e y e s. "This," she said, "is a farewell dinner. A farewell d i n n e r in honor of one whom we all loved, whom we a l l honored. I think he would like it this way better than for us to weep and to wail and mourn him, for he was ever a man of spirit. Will you join me in drinking the health of—Luigi Maroni!"

The health was drunk in silence. She sat her glass down. "Perhaps," she said musingly, "some of you will be interested in knowing that Luigi Maroni had asked me to be his wife." She dropped her eyes, breathed deeply. "And that, my friends, is the reason I am so interested in bringing his murderer to justice. Am I correct in assuming that all of you, friends and admirers of Maroni's, have the same feeling in your hearts?"

If silence meant assent, the entire group wanted, most of all, to hang Maroni's murderer. Amos Carter alone answered. In his harsh, cracked voice he stated that there was no room in Abbottsville for murderers!

"So I've asked an old friend of mine to give us a little demonstration of detective work tonight," she said levelly. "In a few minutes we shall learn many, things of interest concerning the killer of Maroni!"

* * *

Hercules Jones beamed at Doctor Harker. He said, "Lookit, doc, you mean it's okay for me to go dig up this Georgie Vasey and put the muscle on him? And you won't get sore or nothing if I sort of—well—push him around a little?" He was rubbing the spot on his hairless head where his unknown assailant's blow had landed the night before in front of the rear garages at Resthaven!

Harker beamed back at him. "It is quite all right, Hercules, to, as you say, put the muscle on him. I am convinced that he deserves something more than a mere pummeling! But first, you have an errand. You are to take this key to Miss Jeannie, you are to give her this message. Say, 'The bum in jail' and 'Do not forget your promise'. Then, Hercules, you will find Georgie Vasey if you have to sift the town over. And you will keep him securely for me at the cottage. Do you understand?"

Hercules Jones beamed. He flexed his muscles. He went up and down in a rapid squat, like a boxer before the bell. He took the key, marvelled, "And I can teach that lug to quit looking at a guy's middle! Thanks, doc, thanks!"

DOWN in the Blue Room soft footed waiters wheeled in another table, covered by a cloth. They wheeled in a thing that looked like an old fashioned camera, as used by photographers years ago. This and several more objects, including a large box, which was stood on end and covered with a Mexican *serape*. A silence descended over the banquet table. Five pair of eyes peered curiously from the face of their hostess to the apparatus at the far end of the room.

Again Lita Bane came to her feet. "Gentlemen," she said levelly, coldly, accusingly, "there is, tonight, a traitor among us."

Someone dropped a piece of silver, but no one leaned to pick it up. A waiter hovered in the shadow by the door.

"I hardly think," she continued, having been coached by the doctor, "that an attempt will be made to silence me, because the traitor is a coward. Who he is, I do not know at the present time. Very shortly we shall all know, and you men whom he has betrayed, shall deal with him as you please."

She was magnificent, standing there at the head of the table, an avenging angel in a white satin gown, eyes flashing, red mouth twisted bitterly.

"You men," she went on, "with the aid of Maroni, have held this town in the hollow of your hands for years. You have allowed criminals to come to cover here and enjoy immunity from arrest. At a great price to the criminals! You have grown rich in so doing. You have controlled the police and the politicians and the merchants and the publicans." She leaned forward, resting her hands on the table. "Then, suddenly, you did an about face. You ran the criminals completely out of Abbottsville, you told them that no longer could you offer them protection. Why?"

Carson Thames sputtered, "Ridiculous! There's no sense in—"

Amos Carter, the publisher, pushed back his chair, his eyes blazing. "I refuse to sit here and be insulted by this woman—this—!"

The waiter who had been standing in the shadow of the door shoved his chair under him so viciously that he practically collapsed into it.

Luke Melton smiled lazily at the Joan d'Arc at the head of the table. His voice rose above the others. "Words are so cheap—*Miss Sloan*. Proof is a different matter. But go on, your words are interesting—at least."

"You cleaned up the town," she snapped viciously, "because you saw a prospect for more and greater loot! Should I tell you how? You were contacted by the sister of Shag Zachary, the racketeer. Shag Zachary wanted to dispose of great amount of bonds and securities which he had cached. Shag Zachary, the man of mystery! But he insisted on secrecy, he was through with the rackets; he insisted that you run the criminal element out of town. He wouldn't deal until you did!"

There was utter silence in the room, except for the audible breathing of Honest John Chambers, who seemed threatened with apoplexy.

"Shag Zachary," said the girl, "left the penitentiary as scheduled. He went to his cache; he headed for Abbottsville. Where is Shag Zachary, gentlemen? I ask you, where is Shag Zachary? So far he hasn't appeared in Abbottsville!" There was, of course, no answer. Her voice dropped lower. "One man among you knows. *The traitor, who thought to cross up the rest of you!*"

At the word traitor, five pairs of eyes wandered about the table accusingly. The same thought came to each man. Who had pulled a cross?

"One of you," she said dryly, "decided not to be satisfied with a cut of Shag Zachary's remaining wealth. That traitor decided to have it all. Let me tell you what happened. That traitor and his helper rode in a black sedan out of town to intercept Zachary. Their plan was to machine gun him—like Chicago gangsters—and to steal the securities before they ever arrived at Abbottsville."

She reached for a glass of water, lifted it with steady fingers.

"Unfortunately this plan went wrong! Because Doctor Thaddeus Harker, purveyor of *Chickasha Remedies—*"

"And your friend and protector," interjected Melton. For a moment she stared at him.

"And my friend and protector," she said shortly, "happened along when the Zachary car came out of the ditch. However, the Zachary car preceded them to town, where the traitor and his hired killer caught up with it!"

She paused again. Her voice sank low once more. "There is, I say, a traitor among you. You are bold, relentless men, all of you. You will know what to do with the traitor. I introduce you to Doctor Thaddeus Clay Harker."

HARKER stepped through the rear door of the room, approached his paraphernalia, hat in hand. He bowed with dignity, said, "Gentlemen." Again silence overhung the banquet room.

"Gentlemen," he repeated softly, "in my lifetime I have made a study of crime and criminals. I have perfected and improved on several pieces of apparatus since adopted by many cities and states. For example—this." He drew the cover off the apparatus that resembled the old fashioned photographer's camera so closely. "This, gentlemen, I call the Improved Harker Spectograph. It is, commonly speaking, used by scientists to detect the presence of gold, or any other metal, in clay or ore. I have, by combining it with an ultra-violet ray, adapted it for use in criminology. That machine is so delicate that it can detect the presence of a teaspoonful of salt in a hundred thousand gallons of water! It is absolutely infalliable. With it, I intend to prove to the group here assembled, that one of them indeed, is not only a traitor to his colleagues, but a triple murderer as well!"

Carson Thames was on his feet. "Triple murder!" he bellowed. "If you think—"

Doctor Harker raised his hand, transfixed the man with a piercing glare.

"Maroni," he said softly, "was killed with a wire garrotte. Arthur Wallace was killed in a similar manner. I intend to show you another corpse killed by the same diabolical contrivance." He paused. "Murderers," he went on, "run to form. A successful killing by a certain method always warrants another similar killing in the warped mind of the criminal. Crimes are earmarked, as surely and certainly as cattle are branded. Now, gentlemen, suppose you step close to me. With the aid of this apparatus I am about to show you something new and startling in the detection of crime."

They came forward as if drawn by a magnet, and it might have been noted that each man kept well away from his neighbor. The pack was quickly beginning to divide.

"Suppose," said the doctor softly, "with the aid of my spectograph I could prove that one among you was at least *present* at three killings. Three murders took place. The first, in the rear garage of Resthaven Courts. The second, upstairs in this very hotel; the third at the home of Mr. Arthur Wallace. Remember, a spectograph accurately shows the difference between dirt found as close together as two or three yards! Suppose then, that I show irrevocably that one among you was at the garage when the first victim was killed,

that lint from the carpet in the suite upstairs and lint from the carpet in Arthur Wallace's home can also be found on his shoe!"

At the word shoe, he swept the covering off the table. A row of shoes were revealed. Honest John Chambers stared fascinated at the battered Congress gaiter on the very end. With unbelieving eyes threatening to pop from his head. Amos Carter stared at his own black oxford, second in line. Thames reached instinctively for the third shoe, a brown sports oxford, and drew back his hand. The patent leather pump was, of course, Melton's, the sturdy, crepe-soled shoe, belonged to Blitz. The shoe on the end—though they did not know it—was owned by George Vasey.

The pack split! The pack suspicious! The pack wary! Each glared at the other, glared at Doctor Thaddeus Harker, who twisted his moustaches in pleased aplomb.

Hoarsely, shaken out of his blandness, Melton demanded, "And the third corpse, where is it, who is it?"

Harker moved swiftly to the large, upended box. He pulled down the *serape*. The contorted face of Stanley stared out grotesquely at the assembly. "Who—who?" quavered Mayor Chambers, and Harker's jigsaw puzzle fell into place when there was no other comment.

"This," he said sharply, "is Shag Zachary, murdered on his way to Abbottsville!"

There was no dissenting voice among them.

"Standing before me," said the doctor, "is the man who would have betrayed his coterie, his confederates. A man who has killed three times! A man who—"

The lights went out. Brenda Sloan's

scream filled the room, reverberated from wall to wall.

Carson Thames stentorian roar came. "Don't let that faker get away! He probably killed Zachary himself!"

CHAPTER XIII

Gentlemen, to Crime!

OCTOR THADDEUS CLAY HARKER was not one to enter into danger without preparing for all exigencies. B r e n d a Sloan had her instructions, she knew exactly what to do under any circumstances. The scream had been involuntary. She knew, better than the doctor, just how desperately dangerous these men gathered here could be. When the lights went out she screamed for Doctor Harker, not for herself.

Somehow she fought her way, felt her way, through the deep blackness toward the rear of the room. She heard crashes as the instruments exhibited by Doctor Harker rattled to the floor. By hugging the wall she made her way past the struggling men, went through the curtained door and found Doctor Harker pressed tightly against the wall of the passageway waiting.

"Something's wrong," he hissed. "The man on the door—a government man! The lights have evidently been pulled at the main switch, or a fuse blown!"

But as they traversed the black hallway they saw that it was merely a fuse, for the lights were on in the section of the hotel they entered. They went through the kitchen, leaving a wake of surprised cooks and pantrymen, headed for the rear entrance. Brenda paused. "Why not my suite?" she panted. "They'll think we ran out the back door! It'll give us time!"

Up the service stairway they trotted, through the heavy fire-door. The hall turned toward Brenda's suite. Doctor Harker peeped cautiously around it.

"Back," he whispered hoarsely, "there's a cop at the door of the murder suite! He may be Thames' man."

They stood there for a moment, hunted, wondering which way to turn, then turned back. As they passed the fireplace Doctor Harker snatched something from the mantel. Through the fire-door again! They paused at the head of the steps, heard approaching footsteps!

"The service elevator," whispered Brenda, and they made down the hall.

The service elevator was in use. Topless, it rose upward in the shaft, two men, guns in their hands, turning the white pastiness of their faces toward Doctor Thaddeus Harker.

"Back," called Harker, "back down or I'll throw this!"

Melton grasped the cord that operated the elevator. Thames cowered back in the corner. "Godalmighty," he ejaculated, "the fool's got a stick of dynamite!"

The elevator started down again.

Doctor Harker tossed the yellow candle aside, seized Brenda's arm, ran again for the service door. "We'll have to risk the cop," he grated. "Surely the Feds will have it all under control in a minute."

They hastened about the ell of the hall. The cop was gone. A few seconds later, Brenda opened her suite door, rushed in, Doctor Thaddeus Harker close on her heels.

Georgie Vasey came out of the closet, gun in hand. He looked at Doctor Harker's stomach. "What's all the commotion" he growled, "just because I put your damned light out? I been waiting for you. Out in the hall. and walk careful."

Out in the hall again, hurrying down it toward the passenger elevator, "Stop!" screamed a voice. Amos Carter, publisher of the *Courier* came around the ell, gun in hand.

Georgie Vasey turned, shot once, and Carter collapsed.

The trip through the lobby was a nightmare. Behind them they left an unconscious elevator boy, felled by Vasey, and a bellboy with a split scalp who tried to stop them. Then Brenda was at the wheel of the black sedan, Doctor Harker was in the back seat with Vasey's gun boring into him.

"Drive like I tell you," snarled Vasey, "or I let the old guy have it right here!"

She drove very carefully, twisting and turning at command. Once she cut through an alley, once she made a U turn on a boulevard and doubled back the way she had come. Presently, satisfied that they were not followed, he told her where to go. There was nothing to do but obey. Later, Doctor Harker asked permission to smoke. Three times he lit stogies and cast them away as if too nervous to enjoy them. And the last was thrown away before the very door of their destination itself.

BOUND firmly to a chair in the storeroom of the Resthaven Courts, Doctor Thaddeus Harker harangued his captor. Across from him, similarly bound, sat Brenda Sloan. Already his shrewd eyes had taken stock of his surroundings. The storeroom or supply room was in a building to the rear of the garages where the body of Stanley had been discovered by Herk the night before. It was obvious that no call for help would be heard, nor would it be strictly healthy to raise a voice in the presence of Georgie Vasey, whom Doctor Harker already knew as a killer.

Nevertheless he talked, "It's so useless, Georgie," he said in a level tone of voice. "I knew all about it last night, you know. At the party at the hotel tonight the waiters were all G-men, men whom I had sent for through Hercules."

At the words Hercules, Georgie Vasey curled his lip. "That bum," he said, and sneered at the spot where Doctor Harker's belt buckle would have been had he worn a belt.

"Funny," mused the doctor to himself, "the hatred felt by a small man for a larger, stronger person." Aloud, "You can't expect to get away with it. Tests of your shoes showed that you paused on the road where the coupe went into the ditch. Tests likewise showed that you were here in the garage, that you were in the suite where Maroni was killed, and that you were also at Wallace's. Lint from both carpets stuck in the mud on your shoes! And your confederate will accuse you of all these killings."

Georgie said, "Nuts."

Doctor Harker sighed. A second later a key twisted in the lock and a man stepped in. The light in the storeroom was a solitary fifteen watt bulb dangling from the ceiling. Added to that, the newcomer wore a black slicker, a black hat and a handkerchief over his face.

The voice that issued from behind that handkerchief was hoarse and cracked, as if the man whispered, or was afflicted with a cold. "Nice work, Georgie. We'll go to town now."

Doctor Harker said politely, "How do you do, sir? I believe I talked to you on the phone only last night, about five minutes after you and Georgie killed Arthur Wallace?"

The man's heavy breathing could be heard in the little room. His eyes glared at Georgie. Georgie looked at the middle button of the raincoat, said, "Hell, I didn't tell him nothing. He's a wise guy. He knows I was sticking around when all three of them gees was knocked off. Don't you, pop?"

"Certainly," smiled the doctor. Time, time, he was saying to himself. A little time, a little time. "I know much more about this than you think I know. I figured *you* from the start, Georgie, because it was obvious that you were playing a game with Jeannie. I believe you'd just killed Stanley when we registered last night. You knew she'd be suspicious if she saw your wet clothing, but you overlooked your shoes. They were soaking wet."

The hoarse voice said, "Never mind that now. What I want to know is—"

"You want to know where Zachary's securities are, don't you? Sir, I am a very curious and a very egotistical man. Humor me, and you may find out much, try force and you learn nothing."

Georgie said, "Nuts," again.

"Exactly," agreed Doctor Harker. "Now suppose we don't go into detail concerning all the murders, gentlemen. You," he beamed, "you killed Stanley, and suddenly found out—no doubt from his papers—that he wasn't Shag Zachary at all! Shag Zachary was a man of mystery, seldom photographed. The only person in town who knew him was Maroni. I take it that you played all the angles. No doubt you intended to have someone come in, some friend, perhaps, and impersonate the great Zachary a bit later. Consequently, Maroni, who knew him, must die. You probably planned to also murder Jeannie Zachary!"

"Let's go to work," snarled Georgie. "This gripes me."

"Let him finish," said the masked one. "He talks well. We got plenty of time."

"WALLACE died," said the doctor sadly, "because evidently he knew something important to tell me. I can guess that."

"Listen," rasped the man at the door, "suppose you see if you can guess good enough to save your own skin. We know the man we killed wasn't Zachary. But he was driving Zachary's car, the license number checks. What we want to know is what happened to Zachary and all his dough. All his securities. Guess that, old man, and maybe we'll let you live."

"He knows," said Georgie, "he knows too damned much. He's a smart alec. Played like he burned that corpse!"

Doctor Harker said, "Thank you, Georgie. And you're quite a smart alec, too. Putting the corpse in the trailer was okay. It kept Jeannie from finding it, chancing on it. Pretending to burn it simply kept you from searching for it, gave me an opportunity to use it to good advantage tonight."

Georgie leaned over and hit the doctor across the point of the jaw with the barrel of his gun. The room swam, the light seemed to spin in a circle.

When he recovered his complete senses again he saw Georgie Vasey standing over Brenda. Poised over her head was a loop of piano wire, gleaming in the faint light. The man at the door said, "How do you like my gadgets, Doctor? I make 'em myself, but they're not patented. Do you suppose an application of *Chickasha Remedy* would cure your girl friend after it's pulled in place? Guess, doctor, guess! Guess me up nine hundred grand in securities and bonds!"

Brenda said, "Keep still, doctor, a guess won't help. Keep still, they don't dare."

The wire garrotte slid into place. The gleaming bit of steel that was a death trap tightened around her slender throat. Doctor Harker said, "Let me think." But he wasn't thinking, he was listening.

*　　*　　*

At the rear of the storeroom Hercules Jones and three government men paused before the barred window. "Pry it off, or else we'll beat down the door," snapped the first. "They're in there, the cigar butt before the door proves it!"

Hercules said, "And let them blast doc and the girl? Hell no, don't you see they've killed three times already? They can only burn once. No, we got to do it quiet."

His great hands gripped the bars on the window, pulled at them gently. They were the ordinary house protective bars, not round, but flat, strips of steel. He turned partially sideways, he grasped a bar in each hand, more firmly. He crouched. He began to strain there in the moonlight, strained until sweat beaded his forehead, and the veins and cords stood out on his throat like ropes. Slowly, slowly the two bars bent in the middle. Now he reversed, pulling them back together. This time they yielded more easily. In a matter of moments both strips broke in the middle, were bent back out of the way. Pausing only to fling a handful of sweat from his forehead, the strong man grasped the next two strips.

BRENDA SLOAN coughed, gagged. The masked man said, "All right old man, do your stuff. We're desperate, we've killed three times. Look at her face, see her eyes bulging? Another notch, Georgie, and out pops her tongue. Guess, old man. Where's the stuff, where's Zachary?"

Faintly again, from the next room of the storehouse came the sound the doctor had heard before. He said slowly, "Suppose Zachary was riding with Stanley, suppose Stanley was a trusted friend. You fellows pull by and give them the works, but Zachary is on the floor and you don't see him! You stop, there in the road, hear the approach of our car and go on over the hill. You never do see Zachary, but he's there!"

"Go on, go on, talk fast!"

"You said to guess and I'm guessing what I'd do if I was Zachary, with all those bonds, I'd know then that Abbottsville, or someone in Abbottsville, was fixing to cross me. I'd take to the ditch, as soon as the sedan was out of sight, *before our car and trailer came up!* As soon as the tire was changed and the road clear, that is as soon as Stanley and Herk and I drove off, I'd have hidden the briefcase with the bonds. Remember there was a culvert down the road? Why not beneath it?"

Silence for a moment. Georgie said softly, "A guy can't guess like that. How'd he know they were in a brief-case? Let me twist this gadget a bit."

"I think," said the hoarse voice, "he may be telling the truth." A gun appeared in his hand. "I think you can twist as tightly as you please," he went on. "We've all we want from these people now." He raised the gun.

The rear door of the storeroom burst open. A federal man called, "Put them up, mister, and drop that gun." The masked man whirled and shot— at the door. The thud of the bullet into wood was distinctly heard before gun-fire answered him. The gun dropped from his hand, he spun, opened the door and ran. The same gun blasted again, there was the sound of a falling body.

Inside the storeroom the federals pulled Hercules off the fallen Georgie. The big man stood back, disappoint-ment on his face. "Heck," he snorted, "I only got to smack him once before he passed out! I was putting on my best headlock and you guys pull me off!" Then he was with Brenda, who was laughing and sobbing alternately against his thick chest.

The doctor, unbound, arose from his chair and smoothed his moustache. He drew a comb from his pocket, combed his silvery locks nonchalantly. "All's well that ends well," he said briefly and beamed about him. "Now let's go out

and see how badly wounded our other murderer is."

"Melton," snarled Brenda viciously. "I told you he was the brains of the thing."

The doctor shook his head. "Not Melton," he said gently. "Rudolph Blitz. He disclosed enough of his father-in-law's plans to Melton to make it look like Melton was the guilty party, but—"

A federal man came in. Briefly he said, "I got him, through the heart. Dead as a mackerel. Yeah, Blitz."

LATER, in their own cabin, Harker said to the group, "I figured Blitz for several reasons, mainly because Melton had men working for him who would have shot the victims, rather than garrotted them. Then, of course, Melton had an alibi for the murder of Wallace, and it was plain that the same killer killed all three victims. I've known about Blitz for some time."

Brenda said, "Then why the farce at the banquet, doc? Do you realize the risk we ran? You sacrificed your spec-tograph and—"

Doctor Thaddeus Clay Harker said, pouring a glass of bourbon around, "My dear, you forget that our original purpose was to run the Ring out of Abbottsville. I will venture to say that telephone calls will disclose the fact that Carter, Melton, Chambers and Thames are now among the departed. The spectograph," he chuckled, "is a peculiar instrument. It frightens lay-men. While none of them was directly in the murder mud, they doubtlessly had their feet in other mud, up to the ankles. Man instinctively distrusts that which he does not know. They distrust the spectograph, they are afraid of what scientific criminology might re-veal concerning them. And with the

Federal men here and a murder and graft story breaking around their heads— Yes, I am about positive that Abbottsville now needs a new mayor and chief of police!"

Again he chuckled. "As far as the spectograph loss is concerned, the instrument you saw in the Blue Room, my dear, was exactly what it looked like—an old fashioned camera. My real instrument is there in the corner."

"And Zachary? You really think he was in the car with Stanley? That he—?"

Doctor Harker nodded smugly. He extracted an envelope from the breast pocket of the Prince Albert. "A few moments ago," he said, "the porter brought this down from the office. I'll read it aloud."

He cleared his throat, read, "Dear Doctor Harker: You were right, though how you knew is more than I know. Shag has agreed. He will meet Federal men Wednesday at the St. Charles, in New Orleans. Shag has the securities intact. It may interest you to know that he hid them beneath a culvert when he and his friend, Frank

Stanley, were shot off the road. Am enclosing your fee. Best of luck to you and Chickasha Remedies. Jeannie."

And he explained briefly how he had found Shag Zachary hiding in jail as a bum!

"This," he mused, turning over and unfolding the second enclosure, "is a bill of sale for Resthaven Courts, made out to me, in consideration of the sum of one dollar and services rendered. Mmmmmm. Hercules, do you think you could operate a tourist court?"

But Hercules was looking too puzzled to hear. His mind was groping and grasping, reaching out, so to speak. He said, "Lookit, doc, if you don't mind telling, how'd you know this guy Zachary would be holed up in the jailhouse?"

The doctor raised the bourbon bottle, eyed its remaining contents. For a moment he was about to launch into the tale of the ultra successful mule finder, but decided it hurt his standing.

So he shrugged, looked mysterious, winked at Hercules, raised his refilled glass, said, "Gentlemen, to crime!"

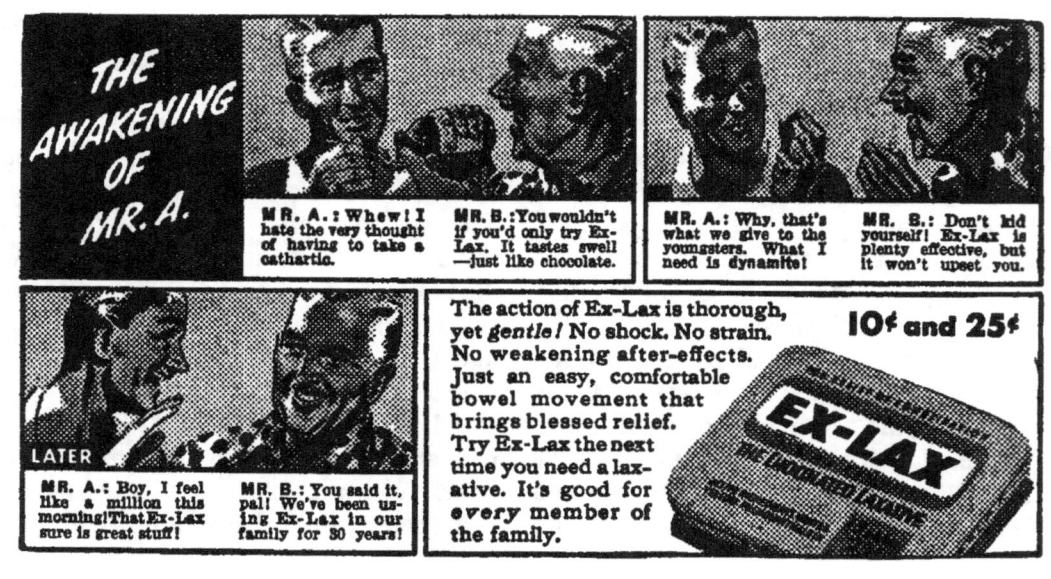

Nick Ransome, proprietor of Risks, Incorporated, finds stunt flying a cinch compared to tracking down a ruthless kidnapper and double murderer

The cabin crate landed with a splintering racket

Peril For Sale

By
Robert Leslie Bellem

CHAPTER I

Murder Crash

MY ALTIMETER clocked six thousand feet when the pursuit ship's pilot began slamming tracer bullets at my two-place cabin job. I juiced my radial Wasp, went into a tight inside loop. Staying in camera range was tricky work, but five years of Hollywood stunting teaches you the angles.

Far below, the Superscreen location ranch was a flat chocolate face flawed by wrinkles that were deep gullies and green pimples that were clumps of trees. Leveling off, I squirmed around to Bonnie Redette. "Time to bail out, kiddo," I said.

There was a queer expression in Bonnie's cat-green eyes, an odd twist to her mouth. If I hadn't known her so well, I'd have sworn she was scared silly. But that was ridiculous. Of all the dare-devils on my payroll—I'm president of Risks, Incorporated—this taffy-haired amazon had the coldest disregard for danger. To see her hesitate over a commonplace jump was as unbelievable as hearing Hitler had knuckled under to Poland.

Her voice was thin and harpstring-taut as she said: "It's no dice, Nick. I can't do it."

To the left, Steve Bullard's camera plane was in perfect position to shoot Bonnie's caterpillar act. "Cripe's sake, Bonnie," I growled. "What's wrong with you?"

She said: "Nero Vaccardi," and her hand went to her mouth. "I didn't mean that."

Before I could pry up the edges of this remark, words blasted my left ear where I had a headphone clamped. It was Bullard, the assistant director, paging me by short wave. "Hey, Ransom, tell that Redette wren we haven't got all afternoon."

I glued the squint on Bonnie, saw she was in dead earnest about not bailing out. The terrified look on her face gave me the creeps. "I simply c-can't make it, Nick," she faltered.

That dumped the matter in my lap. Risks, Incorporated, had made a contract with Superscreen Pix to furnish thrill-footage for this spy opus, and I had a rep to maintain. I switched on my transmitter. "Nick Ransom calling Bullard."

He cut back from his camera plane. "Yeh, we're still waiting."

"Give us four minutes," I said, and snapped him off before he could ask questions. I turned to Bonnie Redette. "Undress, babe."

"Wh-what?"

"I'm pinch-hitting for you," I told her. "You crash the crate and I'll make the leap."

"But the scenario calls for a girl—"

I knew that. According to the script, the heroine was escaping from an espionage ring in a plane piloted by her brother. Overtaken in midair, the brother was supposed to be wiped out. Then the girl bailed out while the ship crashed to destruction. It was hot stuff.

Sylvia Dayle, blondest and brightest star on the Superscreen lot, was this lurid drama's leading lady. Naturally, Sylvia's gorgeous neck was too valuable to risk in a parachute jump, so Bonnie Redette was doubling for her while I wrecked the plane in a dead-stick landing. Later, cabin interiors would be shot in a prop ship on the studio sound stage; closeups would show Sylvia Dayle personally wafting her delectable self overboard, to land on a mattress three feet below the camera line. These closeups would then be matched to the genuine air sequences, with the public none the wiser.

"Sure it's a jane that's supposed to jump," I said. "So what?"

"So you're the wrong gender." Bonnie's counterfeit smile missed conviction by a mile and a half.

I said: "Wearing your duds in a long shot, I'll look enough like a dame to get by. Peel."

"On one condition, Nick. Use your own chute. Not mine."

I blinked. "Are you hinting your umbrella has been tampered with? Don't be dopey. You packed it yourself."

"I know I did. Call it a hunch."

"Okay, sister," I said wearily. "Undress and take the controls. You're not afraid to wash out this tub, are you?"

"No, I'm not scared to do that." Which didn't make sense either. There's a lot more danger in cracking up a plane than there is in a simple bail-out. But she was asking for it.

SHE unzipped her khaki jacket and whipcord skirt. I watched her out of the tail of my eye. She was a husky number, almost as tall as I am, and for a babe in her early thirties she certainly owned a copious collection of contours.

Her skirt and jacket made a dun-colored puddle around her slim ankles. She kicked off her pumps, rolled her sheer stockings down her shapely underpinning.

I slid out of the seat, gave her the stick. I made her fasten two safety belts on her, one around her midriff, one buckling about her chest. I jammed a crash helmet on her taffy hair and said: "Remember to relax when you hit."

"I'll remember, Nick."

I stripped to my shorts, wedged myself into Bonnie's habiliments. I felt funny with my gams in chiffon and my dogs crowded into high-heeled pumps, but business was business. With the parachute harness on my shoulders, I was ready to take off. "All set," I said.

She looked at me; froze to the controls. The plane lurched. "Nick! That's my pack you've got on!"

"To teach you a lesson," I grinned. "You think there's something haywire with your parasol. I'm going to prove you're wrong."

She unsnapped the safety belts, flurried at me frantically, her greenish glims bulged with fear. "Nick, you'll be killed! Nero Vaccardi—"

I blew her a kiss and stepped out into bright space.

It's peculiar when you bail out. No matter how many times you've done it before, you get the all-gone feeling that comes when you ride an elevator headed too fast for the bargain basement. Then there's no sensation at all, except the wind whistling piccolo solos around your ears. It's like being motionless, unless you happen to look down. Then you see the ground leaping at you with too damned much velocity, and you start thinking about your misspent youth.

I counted slowly: "One and two and three," pulled the D-shaped ripcord ring and braced myself for the jerk of the harness when the chute opened. Nothing happened, except that the D-ring came away in my hand. The ripcord had snapped apart.

I yelled: "Hell's breakfast!" and hurled the useless ring away from me. They say a drowning man sees churned montages of his past as he sinks for the final time, but I didn't have any such experience as I plummeted. I was too busy hunting for the busted end of the ripcord so I could pull it.

Pawing like a maniac, I wondered how the hell that cord could have parted. Such things simply don't happen. We check our equipment too often. Unless it could have been sabotage . . .

I remembered Bonnie Redette's terrified refusal to make the jump, her hunch that something might go wrong. And she'd kept mentioning a certain name. Nero Vaccardi.

Nero Vaccardi. What did she know about that guy, and why should the knowledge drain all her courage? True, Bonnie had originally come from Chicago, where Vaccardi once held sway as emperor of the rackets. But surely my ace stunt-woman couldn't have any connection with a mug of his kidney. Moreover, the Vaccardi chapter was closed. Uncle Sam had caught up with the scar-necked slob years ago; salted him away in Alcatraz.

Nero Vaccardi. In one of the recent Sunday blats I'd read that his sentence was shortly to expire; that when he was turned loose, the news would be withheld from general circulation. Too many old-time enemies might be thirsting to slice themselves a piece of his Neapolitan gullet. He had to be protected; the law owed him that much.

Well, nuts to Vaccardi. He couldn't have anything to do with the way I was cannonballing downward. In another couple of minutes they'd be scooping up my remainders in a shovel unless my luck turned. The idea sent sweat drizzling down my pan, especially when I thought of all the phone numbers in my memo book. Who was going to solace my sundry sorrowing lady friends after I became defunct?

. . . My fingers closed on a flapping end of wind-whipped cord. I gave it a savage tug.

The pilot chute went pop! and the main parasol dragged out of its pack, filled itself with sunny Southern California atmosphere. My torso quivered as the harness jerked me to a terrific halt. Now I was floating gently earthward; my heart started beating again.

Presently I hit the ground with a tonsil-jarring thump. I went rolling like a tumbleweed as a puff of breeze filled my chute and started dragging me. My borrowed skirt came up and a cornstalk sliver snagged me in the shorts. I gave vent to an agonized ouch and yanked at the lines to spill the wind.

FROM the private ranch-road nearby, a station wagon whammed toward me. It was a location unit car. It screeched to a stop, tossed coffee-colored billows of loose dirt down my neck. A pair of studio dopes raced over to squash the chute. That halted me.

I was on my face. Somebody fastened the grab under my chin to lift me. I heard a voice I recognized. It belonged to Maurie Kent, director of this spy turkey. Kent was new at Superscreen, along with a cargo of other guys since the outfit had been refinanced ten days before. He was saying: "Superb, Miss Redette! That delayed jump—"

I rolled over, choking. "Thanks for the kind words, only I'm not Miss Redette." I spat out a mouthful of earth and pebbles. All I lacked was the spinach to flavor it.

Kent was a short, dapper bozo with a complexion like bronze and the reddest hair this side of a three alarm fire. "Nick Ransom!" he said. "I thought—"

"So did I, but Bonnie lost her nerve; decided she'd sooner do the crack-up than the bail-out." Then I looked into the sky and yelled: "Hell's breakfast!"

Followed by Steve Bullard's camera plane, Bonnie was diving the cabin job much too fast. Over toward the foothills, a place had been leveled for the crash landing; two cameras were perched on a platform parallel, one panning downward with Bonnie's whooshing descent and the other focused on the spot where she was to hit. Grips, juicers and hams were bunched together, watching. They had something damned breath-taking to watch, too.

I leaped at Kent's station wagon, slid under the wheel. I had to get across the field before Bonnie Redette came in; had to signal her to ease off. Otherwise her crack-up was going to be too genuine. She might be hurt. I kicked the clutch, clashed the gears.

Maurie Kent hooked onto the chariot as I gunned it. Momentum almost jerked his arm out by the roots. He tumbled in alongside me. "What's the big idea?"

I said: "Trouble!" and souped the tripes out of that station wagon. I gave Kent one hell of a wild ride. But it didn't do any good. Just as I applied the anchors at the camera parallel, Bonnie hit.

I piled out of the go-buggy before it had fully stopped. I pelted forward, the packed ground stinging my soles like a hotfoot. The cabin crate landed with a splintering racket, its undergear crumpling, its wings collapsing like breakaway furniture. Ploughed dirt frothed up in a thick black spew as the plane skittered crazily and nosed over.

Somebody screamed. I smelled spilled gasoline, sharp, pungent. I roared: "Bonnie!" and hurled myself at the overturned ship.

Maurie Kent's straight-arm took me in the ribs. He arrowed past me before I could get back in stride, his short legs pumping. I dived after him as flames spread around the wrecked plane's snout.

He bleated: "I'm directing this picture! It's my responsibility!" He gained the plane, jerked its door open, plunged in.

Near me, that scream sounded again. I saw Sylvia Dayle, the star of the opus, tottering across the clearing. She tripped.

I caught her. She was a dainty little dish, all golden curls and baby-blue eyes and lilting curves. She was dressed in a khaki jacket and whipcord skirt to match my borrowed ones; she was supposed to have just landed after her parachute leap, and the script called for her to drag her murdered brother from the wrecked plane. That action was knocked galley-west, now. The crate was afire, the fire spreading. Sylvia wrapped her arms around me. "Mr. Ransom—Nick—who's in there?"

"Bonnie Redette, your double." I tried to pull free.

The blonde cutie clung to me. "God —if anything happens to Miss Redette it will be my fault! She did the job I should have done!"

I said: "Don't be punchy. If anybody's to blame it's Nero Vaccardi." Without stopping to explain that one, I gave her a push that nearly sent her sprawling. Then I started toward the wreckage.

Heat surged at me in waves. I kept going. Then Maurie Kent staggered out of the overturned fuselage with Bonnie Redette in his arms.

She was a hefty burden for a guy Kent's size. His red hair was singed, his lashes and brows scorched short, his map copiously blistered. But he made it.

Then his knees buckled. I grabbed Bonnie away from him and said: "Kent, you may be new around here but you've got nerve."

"Never mind the compliments. Is Miss Redette . . . okay?"

She lay heavily against me, her head lolling at an angle I didn't like. I hefted her up to the camera parallel, mashed my palm against her heart. I couldn't detect any movement there. I began probing at the nape of her neck.

My voice choked when I presently said: "Broken vertebrae. She's dead." I pointed to the bruised place.

Thirty yards down the field, the camera plane came in to a three-point landing. Steve Bullard, the assistant director, ran toward us with his lenshound trailing him. Bullard was awkward, angular. His pasty complexion looked as if it might have originated in solitary confinement, and when he ran his black coat flapped like the wings of a dissolute crow. "What happened?" he croaked sepulchrally.

Maurie Kent mumbled: "God! A fatal accident on my first picture!"

He could call it an accident if he wanted to. But to me, it was something else entirely.

It was murder.

CHAPTER II

Picture Album

SYLVIA DAYLE took another look at Bonnie's corpse and collapsed in a blonde faint. Steve Bullard caught her, cradled her in his embrace. His expression was fifty per cent concern and the rest love in bloom. That surprised me somewhat. I'd been under the impression that the yellow-haired star was pretty sweet on Ben Wisdom, executive head of Superscreen Pix. Maybe Bullard was runner-up for her affections, I decided.

I fastened the clutch on Maurie Kent's arm as the others in the crowd began to mill around. I said: "Better quiet these dopes down, or you'll have a contagion of hysteria."

Kent turned, raised his voice. "Go home, everybody. No more work today. Bullard, you take Miss Dayle back to Hollywood."

She had opened her peepers by then. "Y-yes, Steve. Take me home, please."

Kent added: "Do some telephoning on your way. Notify the authorities and an undertaker."

I butted in, named a mortician friend of mine. "He's the guy I want," I said. "I'll handle the funeral arrangements. Bonnie was my employee, and she didn't have any relatives. I can do that much for her."

The unit slowly scattered. Bullard helped Sylvia Dayle into his coupe, drove off with her. Within forty minutes, a hearse showed up. So did the county cops. I kept my face shut about the murder angle. "Unavoidable accident," I said, and watched as they carted Bonnie away.

Presently it was all over. Maurie Kent told me goodbye, stumbled into his sedan and ordered his chauffeur to drive him to his hotel on Wilshire. I climbed aboard my own bucket—an imported Mercedes, my one concession to Hollywood grandeur—and headed for town.

I stopped at my bungalow, shifted into a fresh set of masculine threads. Then I drove over to the apartment on Franklin that Bonnie Redette had shared with her girl friend, Maureen Trask.

This Trask cutie was a Superscreen bit-player and damned attractive. It was dusk when she opened to my knock. Her violet lamps were red-rimmed, her make-up streaky where tears had irrigated the powder and rouge. "Oh-h-h, Nick. . . !" she whimpered when she saw me standing there.

I walked in. "Then you've heard?"

"Over the radio," she said. She was tiny and wistfully fragile in a negligee of slinky pink satin that rippled like water when she walked. The pink harmonized perfectly with her skin, made her blue-black hair seem even blacker by contrast. "When . . . when I think of Bonnie . . . so alive, so full of energy this morning . . . and n-now she's d-dead. . . !"

I slid an arm around her slender waist. "At least it was quick," I said gently. "She didn't suffer. You mustn't let it throw you, Maureen."

She nestled against me, fragrant and woeful. I liked the faint perfume she wore, the little-girl way in which she cuddled to me. I chucked her under the chin, raised her face. She looked ready to turn on the weeps. Her lips were tremulous.

I planted a kiss on them. A lingering one.

She drew back sharply. "Nick!"

The stunt had worked. She wasn't tearful now. The unexpected impact of my mouth on hers had shocked her back to normal for the moment. Suddenly, for the first time, she seemed to realize that she was in negligee. She blushed, pulled the pink silk together. When a jane is embarrassed, she hasn't got much time to dwell on other matters—like death, for instance.

"I think I'd b-better put some clothes on," she said.

"It might be a good idea. Then we'll have a little talk."

She went into her bedroom, her dainty feet clicking rhythmically in feathered mules. When she closed her door, though, I put rounded curves out of my thoughts. I had a job to do, and I got at it.

The bedroom that had been Bonnie Redette's was on the other side of the apartment. I sneaked into it, started rummaging around. What little noise I made was covered by the sound of Maureen's shower running in the bathroom. That suited me fine. I was looking for something that might link Bonnie with an ex-gangster named Nero Vaccardi; if I found it, I didn't want the Trask cutie to suspect the score. After all, there was no use throwing a scare into her, I told myself. It was funny, the protective feeling I was developing for that little brunette wren. She did things to me.

I pawed through a lot of bureau drawers full of frilly underwear without locating anything important. Then I tried Bonnie's wardrobe trunk. It was locked, but a bent hairpin fixed that. Buried in the very bottom compartment of the trunk there was an old snapshot album.

I flipped it open. I whispered: "Hell's breakfast!"

THE album wasn't entirely devoted to kodak prints. Most of the pages were used as a scrap-book. There were press clippings galore, and all of them were about Nero Vaccardi back in the old Chicago days when he was kingpin of the underworld.

The thing that stopped me cold, though, was a faded snap of the pudgy, scar-necked Vaccardi with his swarthy arms amorously around a Junoesque bimbo a good head taller than he was. The bimbo was Bonnie Redette!

I closed the album. Now I knew for sure that Bonnie had been connected with Nero Vaccardi before he went to the Federal jug. Maybe she'd been his sweetie, judging from their posed embrace in the snapshot. But if they had been sweethearts, why should Bonnie have feared him? Granting that he was already released from Alcatraz, how could he be the cause of her terror that afternoon if he cared for her at all? Why would he have sabotaged her parachute in an attempt to bump her off?

The summing-up was somehow out of focus. And before I could cudgel my brains, somebody cudgeled them for me—with a bullet. From the living room behind me, a silenced gun whispered its hissing beef. I felt a sharp stab of pain through my skull, as if I'd been bopped by a well-honed axe. A hive of hornets buzzed in my ears and the bedroom started to swim around in crazy circles. As if from a great distance, I heard a yeeping feminine shriek and a man's startled swearing.

Then I didn't hear anything more for a while. The floor came up and belted me on the nose. Temporarily, I was all washed up.

When I came drifting out of my pistol-manufactured dreamland I had a headache built for a hippopotamus. There was blood on my skull; gummy, sticky blood, indicating I'd been unconscious long enough to stop leaking. The slug that had been supposed to kill me had merely parted my hair—and my scalp along with it. I was grateful for the thickness of my cranial bones. Stunt-men are supposed to have heads made of cement. Otherwise we wouldn't be stunt-men.

But what about the guy with the faulty aim? Who the hell was he, and why had he tried to burn me down? The answer lay in that old album of snapshots and press clippings concerning Nero Vaccardi and Bonnie Redette.

The album had disappeared.

Then I remembered the brunette Trask chicken; remembered hearing a scream just before I took ether. I wobbled myself upright. "Maureen! Maureen Trask!" I yelped.

She didn't answer me.

I staggered into the living room— and I saw something that frightened the clabber out of me. Maureen's pink satin negligee was a ripped heap on the rug. Her feathered mules were strewn hither and yon. A chair was overturned.

I said: "Hell's breakfast!" and lunged into her bedroom. She wasn't there. She wasn't anywhere in the apartment.

She'd been snatched.

That had to be the answer. She must have heard somebody prowling the flat as she toweled after her shower. Slipping into the mules and negligee,

she had probably come out to investigate. She had seen the intruder and she had shrieked.

Whereupon the unknown gunman must have fastened the grab on her. All the evidence was there. Maureen's fight had been a losing one. The guy had yanked her out of her kimono, forced her to get dressed and leave with him.

But why?

I found out in a hurry. There came a sudden furious pounding on the apartment's front door. Before I could answer, it mashed open. Two plainclothes dicks lumbered over the threshold. Four uniformed squad-car cops followed.

One of the plainclothes dicks was a guy I knew. His name was Ole Brunvig, and he was a homicide sergeant. Ole welded the unbelieving glimpse on me and yipped: "A gh-ghost, b'gahd!"

I pinched his forearm to let him know I was solid substance instead of ectoplasm. "Ghost, hell!" I said. "How come?"

He rubbed himself and cursed. "You're supposed to be croaked! A jane named Maureen Trask just phoned headquarters and said she'd killed you!"

CHAPTER III

Worm Bait

HE MIGHT just as well have biffed me in the teeth. Maureen wouldn't have drilled me. She wasn't the type, and she had no motive for burning me down. It was ridiculous.

I said: "Listen, Swede, I'm not a corpse. You can see that. But I came damned near being one. Some wisenheimer creased me, left me for dead."

"Yeah. The Trask filly. She said so."

"Wrong! Maureen Trask merely caught the guy at it. He must have cracked down on her. You see, he thought he had cooled me off, so he forced her to phone in that fake confession in order to keep suspicion away from himself. Then he kidnaped her."

"Why?"

I pondered that one, and the answer I got made me feel damned queasy. At first blush, you'd thought that the gunman would have murdered Maureen right there in the apartment after compelling her to call in that phoney confession. That way, it might have looked like suicide on her part.

But a spurious suicide is hard to stage, especially on the spur of the moment. One slight mistake and the cops would get wise. My gunner, doping it out this way, must have hit on a better idea. Forcing Maureen to get dressed, and then abducting her, would lend weight to her sham confession. It would leave the impression that she had lammed, was hiding out from the law.

Later the kidnaper could knock her off at his convenience; dispose of her gorgeous body so it would never be found. Then he'd be in the clear—and Maureen would be playing a golden harp with the angels. This was the thought that turned me pea-green around the fringes.

I blurted my theories to Ole Brunvig and ended up by saying: "Whoever this guy is, he came here to glom certain evidence before I could lay my hands on it. When he learned that I had already seen it, he tried to rub me—and he took the evidence away with him, along with Maureen Trask. Now Maureen's behind a carload of eight balls. I've got to get the hell out of here."

Ole tried to stop me, I swatted him aside, raced downstairs to my parked Mercedes. Nero Vaccardi was the man I wanted I was sure, now, that he had been released from stir; that he was the one who had shot me, snatched Maureen Trask. He was the only guy who would have a motive. But finding him was going to be a damned tough assignment. I didn't even know where to begin.

My best bet was probably the Superscreen lot, I concluded. I had a sneaking hunch Vaccardi's trail would point in that direction. First, though I stopped at my bungalow and got a .38 Colt out of my archives; made sure it had a full clip. Its cold weight felt good in my coat pocket.

It was around seven in the evening when I switched off my cylinders in front of the Superscreen Studio main gates. The gates were closed for the night but the watchman knew me, let me in. I parked alongside the two-story administration building and ankled through the entrance.

Maurie Kent and Steve Bullard were in the corridor, just coming out of the presidential suite. Bullard inevitably reminded me of a raven in his black coat, but Kent didn't look as spruce as usual. His blistered puss was smeared with yellow unguent, his singed eyelashes were mere stubs. He said: "Hey, Ransom. I've been trying to get you on your home phone for the last hour."

"Why?"

"Ben Wisdom doesn't want today's accident to interfere with our shooting schedule on the spy pic. He says we're to make that escape sequence tonight—the one where the villains cram you into a coffin and dump you in the water tank over on Sound Stage A."

I said: "Nuts to Ben Wisdom. I'm not taking any baths right now. I'm going in to see that guy. I've got some questions to ask him."

"You mean you're refusing the risk, Ransom?" Steve Bullard croaked at me.

"Just postponing it, pal." I said. I brushed on by, wended my way to Ben Wisdom's door. I walked in without knocking.

Wisdom was a porky slob whose oversized bulk dwarfed the ornate desk behind which he was sitting. He'd been the high mogul of Superscreen Pix for a number of years, and I've never liked him a hell of a lot—although I did business with him whenever he needed me. You can't quarrel with your bread and butter.

He wasn't alone, and I liked his companion even less. Larry Giotto was the outfit's new vice president; according to rumor, he had sunk a stack of money in Superscreen and was responsible for all the new blood around the joint. Maybe that was true, but to me he looked like a ditch-digger with a rush of wealth to the head. Flashy clothes and ten-carat diamonds are okay on some folks, but this Giotto wasn't the type. He was too squatty.

I passed him up with a nod and said to Ben Wisdom: "How's about a little chat—alone?"

Wisdom's four chins q u i v e r e d. "There's nothing to chat about. Where have you been the past hour? We need you on the sound stage."

"I'm not working tonight," I said. "Not on stunts. I'm after information."

"Such as?"

"I'll spill it in private," I said.

Larry Giotto stood up, favored me with a supercilious sneer. "Something tells me you're going to do very little work for Superscreen in the future, Mister Ransom. Maybe you don't realize who I am."

I said: "Sure I do. You're a pain in the neck. Must you be going?"

He took an angry step toward me, but Ben Wisdom's swift glance stopped him. He shrugged and went to the door. "Until later," he said, and beat it.

WISDOM handed me a scowl. "Giotto's the money-man around here, Nick. You should know that."

I gnawed the end off a stogie, torched it. "The hell with Mr. Giotto," I blew out with the smoke. "I've got other things on my mind."

"So have I. There's something I want to ask you, now that you remind me of it. What's this talk you're spreading around regarding Nero Vaccardi being responsible for Bonnie Redette's death this afternoon?"

I stiffened. He could have got that from only one source. I said: "Wait a minute. Have you mentioned this to anybody else?"

"No. But I want to know why you'd link an obvious accident to a man like Vaccardi."

"It wasn't an accident. It was murder," I said. "We'll have more murders, too, if we don't move fast."

"Meaning?"

I said: "Bonnie Redette used to be Nero Vaccardi's sweetie."

If this surprised Wisdom, he didn't show it, except that his fat eyelids lowered and raised again like roller shades. "Well?"

"Let's assume Vaccardi has recently been released from prison. He has a lot of enemies who would murder him if they got the chance. Why? Because they don't want him muscling back into the rackets he used to control. Or because they hate him for all the dirty kills he pulled when he was a big shot. To save yourself, what would you do in Vaccardi's place?"

"Hide out, probably."

"Suppose you wanted to lead a normal life. What then?"

Wisdom said: "I might try to change my appearance so my enemies wouldn't recognize me."

"Go to the head of the class, Ben. Now, let's pretend that was what Vaccardi did. He altered his appearance in some way. Let's also pretend he's living here in Hollywood. Suppose Bonnie Redette saw him and tabbed him in spite of his disguise. That would be easy if she'd been his sweetie in the old days."

"So what?"

I said: "Assume Vaccardi realized he'd been recognized by Bonnie. He might be scared she'd spill to his enemies, lay him open to jeopardy. So maybe he'd try to put her out of the way—by sabotaging her parachute, for instance."

"Nonsense!"

"It's exactly what he did, the way I figure it. Only his scheme happened to miss fire. In the end, though, he got what he wanted. Bonnie was so unnerved by fear that she crashed her plane too hard. Self-destruction induced by terror is murder, in my book."

Wisdom reached for a cigarette. "You talk like a crazy man, Nick. According to you, this Vaccardi thug must be right here in the Superscreen organization somewhere."

"Exactly. He's in this organization under an alias. He tried to bump me tonight, because I was on his trail. And he put the snatch on a filly I happen to like. Now here's what I want from you: I want a list of all the new guys who've been added to the Superscreen payroll during the past ten days— *Hell's breakfast!*" I added in a startled yelp.

Something had come sailing over Ben Wisdom's open transom; something that hissed and sizzled and stank acridly, like burning firecrackers. It landed behind a heavy bank of steel filing cabinets. Sparks and smoke plumed upward.

Wisdom tried to unwedge himself from the chair. "My God—!"

I tore at the cabinets, tried to move them. They were too heavy. I panted: "It's a bomb of some sort. Get out of here fast!" and smashed myself at the door.

It was jammed shut. I couldn't open it.

"The window! Follow me! We'll have to jump for it!" I yelled. Glass crashed when I hit the pane with my shoulder. Sharp shards festooned my air, sliced my cheek. Directly below the window, my Mercedes was parked. I catapulted over the sill, hung by my fingers for an instant and let go.

A stunt-man knows how to fall without busting himself to splinters. You relax when you hit, the way a drunken man does. I landed on my chariot's top, rolled over, smacked the gravel pathway with my hands and knees. I got on my feet, started running.

Over my shoulder, I saw Ben Wisdom trying to scramble over that second-floor windowsill. His bulk teetered there. Then there was an awful blast that seemed to lift the administration building from its foundations. The concussion sent me sprawling. Pieces of wood and stucco rattled through the night like hail.

When I gathered myself together and looked toward Ben Wisdom's window, it wasn't there. Neither was Wisdom. There was just a raw, gaping hole in the wall where his suite had been. Smoke and flames poured out of the hole, like a volcano belching.

Below, my Mercedes was covered with debris. Near it lay a shapeless blob. The blob was Ben Wisdom—what was left of him. Superscreen was going to need a new president. The old one wasn't any more good, except as worm-bait.

A little slower on my feet and I'd have been worm-bait, too. Something told me a murderer was going to be terribly disappointed.

CHAPTER IV

Answer Fades In

THERE was no use trying to salvage the Mercedes. Ben Wisdom was beyond repair, too. A man can't stay alive when his arms and legs have been blown off.

I didn't want that to happen to me. But I knew it might—unless I beat the killer to the punch. The killer, of course, was Nero Vaccardi. But what disguise was he sailing under? How was I going to put the finger on him?

I had hoped to garner some information out of Ben Wisdom, but that was a blind alley now. My next best bet was Sylvia Dayle. The curvaceous blonde star was a damned good prospect, too. Through her, I might narrow down the field of suspects.

My reasoning was simple enough. On location that afternoon I'd told Sylvia that Nero Vaccardi was responsible for Bonnie Redette's accident. I hadn't mentioned the ex-gangster's name to another soul. Yet Ben Wisdom had just hurled the crack back in my teeth a moment ago.

Nobody but Sylvia Dayle could have repeated my suspicions to Wisdom. His death eliminated him from the equation. Therefore, Sylvia must have blabbed my remark to someone else beside the Superscreen president.

That someone else had to be Nero Vaccardi in disguise. By telling him what I had said, Sylvia had put me in the grease up to my elbows. Along with Maureen Trask.

When I thought of Maureen I got the jitters. Maybe she'd already been killed. Maybe—

"Hell's breakfast!" I told myself. "I've got to see the Dayle bimbo; find out who she spilled her dope to. Then I'll be on my way!"

Studio watchmen were running toward the administration building with fire extinguishers. An alarm bell began clanging. Off in the distance a siren sounded. I spotted a sleek Cad phaeton up near the main gates; raced for it. When I got closer I tabbed the "L. G." monogram on the side panel. It was Larry Giotto's heap.

I thumbed my mental nose at the flashy Superscreen vice-president and helped myself to a slice of his horsepower. He probably wouldn't like the idea of lending me his equipage; but as long as he wasn't around to tell me no, what difference did it make?

The ignition key was in place. I twisted it, got the motor going. I headed for the gates. They were open, waiting for the fire engines. I went slamming through them to the street; aimed myself for Sylvia Dayle's lavish Beverly residence.

Luck was with me. I didn't encounter any motorbike cops, and I didn't maim any luckless pedestrians. I scared hell out of a couple, though. Then, presently, I was thumbing Sylvia's front doorbell.

A nifty little number in a maid's uniform opened the door. "Yes, sir?"

"I want to see Miss Dayle," I said.

"She has retired for the night, sir. She had a severe shock this afternoon, and—"

I put my hand on her chest and shoved. "This is important," I said, and made for the stairs. I took them three at a clip.

The servant-girl's yelp helped a lot. It brought Sylvia Dayle to her boudoir portal; saved me the trouble of looking for the right room. Sylvia said: "Why, Mr. Ransom!"

Dim pink light was behind her, and she was wearing a nightie three degrees thinner than a butterfly's whisper. It just happened that at that moment I wasn't interested in glorified anatomy.

"I want to ask you something, baby," I said, pushing her back into the room and following.

Her baby-blue eyes didn't look so babyish when she narrowed them. "Get out of here!"

"Not yet. Listen: You remember today, out at the location ranch? When I told you it was Nero Vaccardi's fault if anything happened to Bonnie Redette?"

"Yes, I remember that. I didn't quite understand it. I don't understand it now. And I don't understand why you should come here and—"

I said: "Skip it. You passed my remark on to some other people. Who were they?"

She blinked. "Why—nobody except Ben Wisdom."

"You're a liar," I said.

Her palm flashed up, whapped me across the cheek. "You can't talk that way to me. Get out of here!"

"Talk!" I said. "Talk before I shake your brains loose."

She wailed and tried to claw me. When she kicked me in the shins it didn't hurt, because she was barefooted. Her raised knee could have done me a lot of damage, though. I twisted away from it, tightened down on her shoulders, shook her again.

"Damn you—let me g-go!" she yowled.

"I will when you tell me what I want to know, baby. Otherwise you're in for a bad time."

THE closet door opened, over on the other side of the room, and a man's voice said: "That's what you think. Turn her loose, Ransom, before I put a bullet in you."

My fingers unclenched a little. Sylvia Dayle jerked free. She dived for the bed, pulled the mussed counterpane up around her. "Go ahead and shoot him, Steve!" she snarled.

I turned around and saw Steve Bullard standing there. He was covering me with a .32 mail order revolver. His eyes looked mean.

I said: "So that's the score. I didn't know I was butting in on a tryst."

"One more crack like that and I'll let you have it, Ransom."

"Wait a minute," I said. I fastened the stare on him, paying especial attention to his pasty pallor that reminded me of solitary confinement. It suddenly dawned on me that he was comparatively new at Superscreen; that nobody seemed to know very much about his past, prior to his Hollwood advent. In fact, a few eyebrows had been lifted when he got an assistant directorship the day he hit town. All of which might spell anything—or nothing.

I studied his lamps. They were ice-gray, glittering. He wore an old-fashioned high choker collar that came up close under his chin, almost matched the floury quality of his puss. A scar might be hidden under that collar; a scar like the one Nero Vaccardi had. Not having x-ray eyes, I couldn't tell.

But there was one thing I could be sure about. That gun in his fist was a damned nasty menace to the safety of one Nick Ransom, stunt-man. Something had to be done about it. Quick.

I flashed a sidewise glance at Sylvia Dayle on the bed. I beeped: "Sylvia—don't do that!"

Bullard took his attention away from me for a split instant. That was all I needed. I sailed at him with all flags flying.

When he realized I'd tricked him, he tried to gun me. I was too previous for him. I bashed the mail order revolver out of his hand, sent it clattering across the room. Then I prescribed some knuckles for his chalky jaw.

The prescription jarred him to the kidneys. He said: Glmph! and his knees sagged. I caught him, held him. "Don't make me do it again," I said. "The next one might damage both of us. I need a good pair of hands in my profession. I'd hate to ruin them on your map."

Sylvia was out from under the covers, reaching across the foot of the bed to stab me with her fingernails. "You let Steve alone! He's my husband and you haven't got any right to—"

"Your husband?"

"Yes! So why shouldn't he be here in my room?"

I was beginning to catch on. "How long ago· were you married, babe?"

"Years ago. When we were both on the stage in New York."

I said: "So after you hied yourself to Hollywood and became a movie star, you sent for Steve. You sugared Ben Wisdom into giving him a job as assistant director. Right?"

She started to nod. By that time, Bullard had all his buttons back and counted. He croaked: "Damn you to hell, Ransom! If you so much as hint there was anything wrong between Sylvia and Wisdom, I'll break your lousy neck with my two hands!" Then he wrapped his fingers around my gullet before I could stop him.

He had a lot of strength. The blood began to pound and roar like surf in my ears. He bent me backward—

When you're a stunt-man you have to be an acrobat, among other things. I let myself go momentarily limp. Then I flipped into a reverse somersault. The somersault slammed Steve Bullard over my head. He lost his grip on my aching throat; wound up against the far wall. His crash-landing put him out for the count.

I looked at myself in the vanity-table mirror, scowled at the bruises on my windpipe and neck. Then I said: "Thanks, pal," and started for the door.

Sylvia flurried off the bed; blocked me. "Where are you going?"

"To put the thumb on a murderer. Your hubby just throttled the answer into my dome. One side, babe."

"W-will you promise not to say anything about—about my being married? It might hurt my career . . ." She was tempting me with her blue eyes, trying to buy my silence with her parted lips.

But I wasn't having any, thank you. I kept thinking of Maureen Trask and of Bonnie Redette as I'd last seen her: dead, her head lolling at a grotesque angle, her throat marred by bruises. That mustn't happen to Maureen, I told myself. Not if I personally had to kill Vaccardi.

I knew his identity, now; knew his plans and guessed his methods. Steve Bullard wasn't connected with the matter, except insofar as he had triggered me into adding up the truth when he assaulted me. Sylvia was equally innocent of complicity. Her guilt, if any, was only of the boudoir variety.

I put my hands under her arms,

lifted her aside. "Save your wiles for the next president of Superscreen," I said. "Maybe you'll be able to buy your hubby a real job." Then I lunged downstairs.

There was a phone in the lower hall. I dialed Ron Carnohan, a sound-technician friend of mine who worked for one of the major lots. I said: "Listen. Can you spare up some sort of portable rifle—mike setup with batteries and a playback—and do it quick?"

"That's a big order. I think I can fill it, though."

"Then make it snappy." I told him where I wanted the stuff; rang off. Then I dialed the Hollywood police division. "Sergeant Brunvig," I said

Presently I heard: "Brunvig talking."

"This is Nick Ransom. I know who bombed Ben Wisdom. It's the same guy that caused Bonnie Redette's death; the one who snatched Maureen Trask."

"Can you prove it?"

"No. That's the hell of it," I said. "But if I work a certain scheme, you'll have all the proof you need."

"Who, what, why and where?" he asked me suspiciously.

I said: "Know where Larry Giotto's house is? Meet me there as fast as you can cover the mileage." Then I hung up and pelted out to Giotto's Cad phaeton. It seemed funny to be using his car on a mission like this. But he didn't know it, so it didn't make any difference.

———

CHAPTER V

Playback to a Fade-Out

THAT sleek heap had a world of speed. I used all it owned. Giotto was living in an elaborate rented house just off Sunset; a house that belonged to a former star of the silent days, now down on his luck. You might have found a more pretentious pile of stone and stucco somewhere or other, but I doubt it. The place had everything, including two swimming pools. I knew. I'd visited there many a time, years ago.

Ole Brunvig was just pulling to a stop in front of the driveway as I skidded up behind him. I ran to his police sedan, dragged him out. "I hope you've got bullets in your gun," I said. "You may have to spend them."

He wanted to dagger a lot of questions at me but I corked him off. "Save it until Ron Carnohan gets here," I told him.

"Ron Carnohan? Who's he and what's he got to do with it?"

I said: "I'm betting all my chips on his dice. If he fails me, I'm sunk. I wish to gahd he'd hurry."

The minutes were snails on crutches. But after a while, my sound-technician pal showed. He had a whole damned sedan full of equipment. "You carry the mike," he told me. "I'll bring the play-back recorder and unreel the wire. The battery is in the car. What's the play?"

I picked up a gadget that looked like several rifle-barrels bound into one. It was a microphone, made especially for picking up sound at a distance, concentrating it, excluding extraneous noises. "Around here," I said, making for the side of the house. "Quiet."

Having been a guest in the joint several times, I was familiar with its layout. The upstairs and downstairs windows on that side were all closed, dark, the blinds drawn. But I knew what the rooms were. That helped.

I set the rifle mike on its portable standard; aimed it. With Carnohan's headphones clamped to my ears, I began directing the tubular contraption first at one window, then another. Now that I was actually trying out my plan, I began to have misgivings. In the final analysis, I'm no sleuth. I'm just an ivory-headed stunt expert with more brawn than brains. Suppose my theory proved wet?

It couldn't be wet, I argued. Vaccardi and Giotto spelled murder, the way six and seven make thirteen. If any other number came up, I was in a filthy fix—and Maureen Trask was in a filthier one. Buck fever got me. I began to shiver and twist.

"Now what happens?" Ole Brunvig asked me.

I kept swinging the muzzle of the microphone at various windows. Suddenly I grabbed Brunvig's arm, handed him one of my two earphones. "Listen!" I whispered. To Ron Carnohan I said: "Get your recorder going, quick!"

He had a wax platter on a portable turn-table. He set it in motion, got the needle in its groove. "What is this, anyhow?"

"The voice of Nero Vaccardi, alias—" I didn't finish the sentence. I was too busy with my electrical eavesdropping.

In a room behind the window at which my mike was aimed, two guys were talking. One complained: "Why make me handle the Trask babe, chief? You took care of Bonnie and Wisdom and that snoopy Ransom mug. Another bump won't upset your conscience."

"Hardly," the second voice chuckled. "But this happens to be your old Chicago specialty. All you have to do is take her to the ocean, slug her unconscious, tie a weight to her ankles and toss her in the drink. Better get started."

My sigh of relief sounded like a steam whistle. Maureen was still alive! Nothing else counted. She was alive, and in this house, and they were planning her murder. I wasn't too late to stop them!

I flipped off my earphones, gestured Ron Carnohan to stop his recorder. "Bring it along for a play-back," I whispered. Then, to Brunvig: "You carry master keys, or is that just a trick reserved for a dime novel dicks?"

"I have a few. Maybe I'm a dime novel."

We reached the front door. He worked on the lock. It opened. We barged in.

I knew the room I wanted. I made for it. Light leaked around a closed door at the end of the hallway. Someone was saying: "I'll be the biggest shot in the movies just like I was in Chi. After I take over Superscreen I'll start expanding. Nobody's ever going to know I used to be called Nero Vaccardi—"

I bashed myself at the door. It splintered, broke open. I slammed into the room and said: "That's where you're wrong, Vaccardi—*alias Maurie Kent!*"

THE phoney director's blistered face went redder than his dyed hair. He leaped upright, whirled toward Larry Giotto on the other side of the room. "You told me my apple bumped this rat!"

"Listen, chief," Giotto bleated. "I thought—"

"You thought wrong," I said. "It missed me. Take them, Ole."

Kent-Vaccardi suddenly had a gun in his hand. He snarled: "You crossed me, Giotto," and pumped three quick pills through the flashy Superscreen vice president's middle.

Ole Brunvig's service revolver started chattering before Giotto hit the rug. Its blamming thunder almost deafened me. The first slug took the fake director's automatic out of his fist, along with a couple of fingers and a thumb. The second caught him in the chest, slammed him against the wall. The third shattered his left kneecap. He went down, writhing like a gaffed eel.

I said: "We saw him kill Giotto just now, so we won't need the play-back for evidence of his confession on the other murders. Maybe he won't live long enough to stand trial. I hope not."

"You . . . stinking . . . son!" the wounded man gasped at me

I torched a stogie, blew smoke in his twisted face "Here's the story: As Nero Vaccardi you were in danger of death the instant you left Alcatraz. So you quit being Nero Vaccardi and became Maurie Kent. Prison thinness and red hair-dye fixed that.

"But you still had a maniac yen to run things. Chicago was out, so you picked Hollywood. Using your old pal Giotto as front man, you invested dough in Superscreen; Giotto went in as vice-president while you played third fiddle as a director. Later you planned to squeeze Ben Wisdom out; move Giotto up a notch. When the time came, Giotto could step aside and you would take over. The thing would look so natural that nobody'd suspect the truth."

He coughed up blood, cursed me with glazing eyes.

I said: "Then Bonnie Redette, your former Chicago girl-friend, recognized you. You were afraid she might spill your identity, so you had to bump her. First you sabotaged her parachute, but that didn't work because I used it instead and managed to get it open. I should have suspected something smelly

when you tried to lift me by the neck after I landed. Remember choking me—until you saw you had the wrong victim?"

He just glared but I knew he remembered.

I went on: "I realized the truth tonight when Steve Bullard tried to break my neck with his bare hands, up in his wife's boudoir. I woke up to the fact that a man could commit murder by snapping his victim's vertebrae. It was what you did to Bonnie Redette; I should have guessed it when I saw the bruises on her throat, because if her neck had been broken by the smash-up, there wouldn't have been any bruises at all. Therefore, it had been done by somebody's fingers.

"But I didn't get it, at the time. I thought fear had made her crash the plane too hard; fear of Nero Vaccardi. Then, tonight, Steve Bullard put me wise when he tried the neck-breaking stunt on me. Comparing my throat-bruises with Bonnie's, I realized she had been killed by human hands—*and you were the one who went into the plane to 'rescue' her. The only one who'd had an opportunity to snap her vertebrae!*

"Which also meant that you were Nero Vaccardi, the guy she'd feared. I could see it clearly enough then. I could see that you were the man who went to Bonnie's apartment, looking for anything that might connect her with you. Finding me there first, you tried to bump me. You stole the album. Then you snatched Maureen Trask because she caught you in the act. To cover your tracks, you forced her to phone in a fake confession."

"You . . . smart . . ."

I blew more smoke "Later, it must have startled hell out of you to see me still alive in the Superscreen administration building. It caused you to have another try at me, this time with dynamite—because you were afraid I knew too much. The dynamite missed me. I went to Sylvia Dayle's house, had that run-in with Bullard. And as I've said before, it tipped me to the truth."

Ole Brunvig stared at me. "One thing I don't understand. How did you dope it out that you'd find him here in Giotto's joint?"

"Well," I said, "I knew he had to be the one who'd kidnaped Maureen. I also knew he lived in a Wilshire hotel where he couldn't take a snatch victim. Giotto's house was the only other answer, since he and Giotto were in cahoots." I looked down at the disguised Vaccardi. "Wasn't I right?"

He didn't answer me. He couldn't. He was meat for the morgue by that time.

So I went hunting for Maureen; found her in an upstairs room, roped to a big four-poster and gagged so she couldn't scream. I pulled the gag from her tremulous mouth, cut her fetters. She put her arms around me and whispered: "Nick . . ." and lifted her mouth to mine.

Well, hell's breakfast. The least I could do was take her home and soothe her. Besides, I've always got room in my memo-book for one more number.

Another Nick Ransome story coming in the next issue of

DETECTIVE DIME NOVELS
— ON SALE AT ALL NEWSSTANDS —

Tom Henderson had a good memory and a gnawing hatred, both of which things helped him find his pal's killers

His hard brogans caught the rickety table and sent it crashing

Trouble for Three

By Murray W. Mosser

THE slanting rays of the afternoon sun played across the cool green and spotless white of the Sunnydale Cafe. An enormous man with a head like a billiard ball and no neck at all sat at the counter gulping down food. It was Kickapopoulis' first meal in three days.

He looked up and smiled contentedly over a great hunk of pie. "Thees town, she has a fine law," he said. "Looking what she's done for me. She's rescue me from getting beat up; then she's feed me before send me to jail."

Mary Duncan sniffed disdainfully, not looking at the hungry one. Her stormy eyes glared disapproval at Officer Thomas Henderson.

"Listen, Tom!" she said grimly. "You spend half your salary to feed every bum that hits town. I'm warning you! You've got to make a choice between," she paused dramatically, "between me and—and people like him."

Tom Henderson reddened under his tan. "Aw, Honey. You know how that jail food is and this poor guy was hungry.

"It's no wonder a crook stays a crook," he finished bitterly. "Nobody gives him a chance to be honest. It's all right for these big city cops to say 'Once a crook, always a crook,' but it don't work in a place like Sunnydale."

"Chief Bass used to be a big city cop," Mary pointed out. "And my brother Dave tells me he's pretty sore at the way you work to get these crooks paroled and back into circulation. I don't like it, Tom. I can't help but feel you may be getting a potential murderer out of the pen. One slip from one of them and you'll lose your job and your friends."

"Wotsa thees," the gigantic Kickapopoulis cut in, wiping his mouth with the back of a ham-like hand. "Thees wan fine mans. You're goin' to marrying him, no?"

Mary Duncan, eying the quizzical expression on the massive face, laughed suddenly. For Henderson it was like the sun coming out after the storm.

"You're darn tootin', Kickapopoulis," she said. "Where else would I find another like him, with the heart of him big enough to fill out his tough hide? Where did he pick you up, anyway?"

"I took the monkey away from three brakemen who were working him over with clubs," Henderson cut in uncomfortably. "The law says I got to lock him up for vagrancy."

He glanced ruefully at his mud-spattered uniform. "I was just coming down to show you my new unifo—"

The viciously penetrating clang of the bank alarm cut into his words. For a moment he stood there looking from Mary to Kickapopoulis and then the air was split by the explosion of gunfire and an agonized scream. Henderson headed for the door, tugging at his gun.

"Whoosa gon' taking me to jail, hah?" Kickapopoulis cried.

"Go down and find yourself a nice, comfortable cell," Henderson flung back over his shoulder.

A crowd was gathering at the bank doors, half a block down the street. He saw another blue-coated figure rushing toward the bank from the opposite direction. That would be Dave Duncan, Mary's brother. Henderson felt a warm, tight inner glow. Between Tom and Dave there existed a bond of friendship that needed no sentimental, gushing statements to confirm it. It was cemented more solidly by their mutual love for Mary.

Several men, guns in hand, backed out of the bank into the street. The majority of the crowd scattered for cover like a fresh-flushed covey of quail, but some of them stood rooted to the sidewalk, too terrified to move.

This latter group made shooting impossible. Too much danger of hitting some of them. Henderson could see that Dave was having the same trouble on the other side.

Henderson cursed savagely and began elbowing his way through the crowd. He reached the fringe of it in time to see one of the bandits line an automatic on Dave Duncan. Henderson snapped up his own revolver.

His mind had already given the order to fire when a hysterical bystander, crazed with fear, started swinging his fists wildly, blindly, in a mad effort to escape from the scene. One of the flailing fists struck Henderson on the elbow, numbing his arm, and the gun dropped from his nerveless fingers. He heard the roaring explosion of the bandit's automatic and watched horrified as Dave crumpled to the sidewalk.

The snarling bandit whirled savagely. Over the cannon-like mouth of the automatic Henderson recognized the hooked, predatory nose, thin features and cruel blazing eyes of Killer Carmen, wanted in twelve states for murder and robbery.

Henderson dove forward desperately. His head seemed to explode internally, with a fireworks display that was his own private world's fair. He couldn't even remember hitting the sidewalk.

HE SAT up to find the blood pouring into his eyes. He freed them with a double-handed swipe of his fingers, felt the long bullet gash in his forehead. He winced and the pain helped bring back the memory of what had occurred.

His eyes sought Dave Duncan. A surge of horror welled over him. He felt his features contort with shock and sudden grief. A trace of moisture came into his eyes and mercifully blurred the ghastly picture.

The bandit's bullet had ripped the top from Dave's head.

Henderson began to breathe hard, like a boxer who has stayed too many rounds. And with each breath he felt his nose draw thin and his nostrils flare slightly. His face felt hard and cold, as though it had been sculptured out of solid ice.

His lips seemed stiff as sole leather as he said aloud in a strained, metallic voice he hardly recognized as his own,

"They got you, Davey. They got you, damn 'em! But God help 'em when I get my hands on them!"

It wasn't until he heard the roar of a motor and a startled cry, "Hey! Dat cop ain't dead!", together with the slap of a slug on the walk beside him, that he realized he had been out only a few seconds.

The bandit car whirled from the curb. Henderson's eyes searched wildly for his gun, located it a few feet away. He scrambled toward it, snatched it up and sent three shots after the bandit car as he came to his feet.

He heard the sirens in the distance then. Too far away to do any good. The murdering rats would get away.

They would like hell! He pumped his legs desperately toward his own car, parked a few yards away, reloading his revolver as he ran.

There wasn't a soul in sight on the streets as he swung out and lined after them. He was five blocks behind, but the motor under the battered hood was deceptively powerful and tuned to perfection.

They hit the open highway moments later, with the wail of the sirens growing fainter behind. He knew that if the bandits found out that he was alone it would be as easy as picking cherries—for them. They'd slow down and turn that chopper on him and he'd look like canned dog food when they got through.

He tromped harder on the accelerator.

A thought struck Henderson and his eyes narrowed. There was an intersection about twelve miles ahead and it would be blocked by only two motorcycles officers of the State Patrol. They wouldn't have a chance against the machine guns in the bandit car.

He had to take them before they hit

that intersection! He set his jaw grimly and pressed the accelerator to the floor-boards. The motor under the battered hood rewarded him for the excellent care given it with an additional burst of speed that carried him slowly closer to the car ahead.

The back window of the bandit car disappeared and the barrel of a tommy-gun wiggled through. Henderson was suddenly conscious of a shortness of breath and a tight feeling in his throat. He gripped the steering wheel with fingers like steel clamps.

Flame danced from the ugly snout of the machine gun and the windshield dissolved in front of his eyes. A sharp pain lanced his forehead and blood ran into one eye. He cleared it with a savage shake of the head, reached up and jerked a sliver of glass from beneath the skin.

He had a strange sense of unreality, as though it were all a fantastic, crazy dream. He laughed suddenly, a hard, bitter laugh. But he couldn't laugh away that flaming tommy-gun.

He pressed the accelerator until his foot ached. The bandit car seemed to melt toward him. He realized they had discovered he was alone and were slowing up to shoot it out.

The rushing wind tore at him and he shuttered his eyes against it. An icy coldness settled over him. Their tommy-gun ammunition was evidently exhausted, and he paid no attention to the angry zip of the pistol bullets. He was holding his fire, knowing he would have no chance to reload.

He drew even with the back of the bandit car, raised his revolver slowly, deliberately. Then he lowered it again without firing. An incredulous feeling of amazement swept over him. He thought for a moment his eyes were playing him tricks.

Mary Duncan was sitting in the back seat of the bandit car, her hands clasped rigidly, her eyes swollen, red-rimmed pools of terror!

Henderson could think of only one explanation of Mary's being with them. She must have seen her brother fall and had run to him while Henderson was out. Carmen had seen an excellent opportunity to obtain a hostage.

Until this moment Henderson hadn't been afraid. His grief and rage had been too tough an armor for fear to penetrate. But now he felt as though a hand were at his throat, choking him.

He made his decision in a flash and swung the wheel sharply to the right. It was going to be nice and tight, but, this way, Mary and he at least had a chance.

All hell seemed to break loose and Henderson caught a glimpse of the stark fear that took charge of Carmen's features.

"Yellow dog!" Henderson thought disgustedly. "The color leaks out all over these tough killers when they get in a jam."

Then his mind was wiped clean as a slate as the sound of grinding, crashing metal nearly ruptured his eardrums. Locked wheels made the two cars buck like broncs.

The sidelashing of his light coupe nearly snapped the neck from Henderson's shoulders. With a terrific whipping motion the coupe broke free and spun toward the opposite ditch. Its front wheels hit the soft dirt and it nosed over like a crashing plane. The ground seemed to come up and smack him in the face, and the black earth to flow over his head.

HENDERSON'S first conscious thought was that he was having a nightmare. Chief Bass' face seemed to float toward him, then fade away. He closed his eyes again and let the world settle down a bit, then opened them.

No doubt of it. It was Chief Bass, all right. And Bass looked like a bottled-up bomb of rage, looking for some place to explode. The veins of his face were so congested that they gave it a purple hue. He was actually trembling.

Henderson eyed the chief ruefully. "Looks like they got away," he said.

"You damn dirty louse!" the chief snarled.

"Huh?" Bass' vicious voice drove the fog from Henderson's brain the way a high wind dries fog from the sea.

"You're in with them," Bass accused grimly. "You lousy rat! I'd like to kill you myself! Dave Duncan dead back there on the sidewalk. Two good men dead in the bank. Four of them all told, counting that skunk Smooty Schultz. And old Jeeter, the bank president, dying in the hospital!"

"So I'm in with 'em?" Henderson's voice was bitter.

"Sure. You—pampering and hobnobbing with crooks the way no self-respecting cop would ever do! I know you got Smooty Schultz paroled from the State Pen, and Smooty was the finger man on the job. One of the tellers shot him and his own pals finished him off like the double-crossing rats they are. As far as I'm concerned that makes you guilty as hell!"

Henderson felt the blood drain from his face. "Smooty—did—that?" he asked hoarsely.

He felt suddenly deflated and soggy, like a wet balloon. His chin dropped forward on his chest and he didn't have the strength to raise it.

If Smooty had thrown in with the bandits it meant the end of everything

for him. The end of his job on the force. The end of his dream of making honest men out of crooks. And, worst of all, the end of his hopes with Mary. The agonizing thought that she would always be thinking that if he hadn't got Smooty out of the pen her brother would still be alive, struck him like a cold knife. She would hate him for that.

The evidence was damning against him. He hadn't fired a shot to save Dave. And he had gone out of his way to befriend Smooty, to pal around with him and try to make an honest man of him. But they wouldn't call it that. He could hear them say, in their inimitable, small-town manner, "Birds of a feather—"

"You—Pete—Jonesy!" the chief snapped viciously. "Jug this damned rat. Get him behind bars and then try to pick up the trail of that bandit car."

The chief's words set Henderson's brain on fire, snapped his chin from his chest. If they ever got him in jail his chances of saving Mary would be nil!

He swung weakly for the chief's jaw, but the blow was so lacking in power that it only made Bass mad. Pete's sap brought blackness once more to Henderson's tired brain.

"Hell!" Henderson thought as he gained consciousness in front of the jail. "This is getting to be a habit." He took inventory with his fingers. A bullet crease and two large and painful lumps on his head. He cursed bitterly.

Music from the sandwich stand across the street cut through the twilight. He got out and walked stiffly between the two men to the jail.

"Shep!" Pete called. "Shep! You around?" Then, "Where the hell is that damned jailer? Whenever there ain't any prisoners in the jug he's harder to find than a flea on a French Poodle."

"Probably out getting coffee," Jonesy grunted. "Well, I know where the extra keys are. Let's lock this skunk up and get going."

Henderson sank to the cot as the door clanged behind him, and dropped his aching head into his big hands. He tried to think and found it a tough proposition. The thought of Mary in the hands of Killer Carmen was like a hot flame searing his brain.

He stood up suddenly and pincered great chunks out of the air with his fingers, wishing it was Killer Carmen's throat instead that he held between them.

The music from the radio in the sandwich shop across the street cut off suddenly and he heard an announcer bawl, "We interrupt this program to bring you the latest bulletin on the Sunnydale Bank robbery. Highway intersections 3 and 26, 7 and 34, 8 and 21 were bottled up immediately after the robbery, and the blockading officers report that no cars have been allowed to pass through. Smooty Schultz, a local youth, who recently obtained a parole from the State Penitentiary with the aid of Police Officer Thomas Henderson—"

A blinding light flashed in Henderson's brain. The intersection of Highways 8 and 21 was the crossing the bandits had been heading for. And there were no side roads leading off between the place where the wreck occurred and that junction point! They couldn't have turned back, or the chief would have seen them. That meant they were still on this side of the highway intersection.

An idea flashed suddenly in his mind and the sense of it made his jaw drop. He breathed in an enormous hope and liked the taste of it. By God! he thought: It's too good to be true!

FIFTEEN years before, he and Smooty and all the other town kids had done their swimming in Moon Hill River, that ran through the bad lands. Since the Municipal Pool had been built, no one went there any more. There had been a road at the time, and an old, abandoned trapper's cabin. If he remembered right, a fence now stretched across where the old road had been. But that would be simple; all the bandits would need would be a wire cutter and some staples.

Henderson leaped for the door and yelled, "Hey! I've got to get out of here! Hey!"

He shook the bars and the noise reverberated in the narrow corridor and sounded like a clap of thunder in his ears.

"Quiet, pliss! How you thinking pipple should sleep?"

Henderson whirled, made out a huge form rising from a cot in the semi-darkness of the cell opposite his.

"Kickapopoulis!" he cried.

Kickapopoulis rubbed sleepy eyes with a hand like a whole hog. "Hah?" he said, peering through the gloom. Then his face lit up.

"Ho!" he boomed happily. "It iss my frien' the law, no?"

"How the hell did you get here?" Henderson snapped.

A puzzled frown creased the billiard-ball forehead. "Now you should telling me I don't belong here! You telling me go fin' a nice comfortable cell. I come here. Thees man telling me I can't come in—"

"WHAT man?"

"Thees man." Kickapopoulis reached down and pulled a bound and gagged figure from beneath the cot. Henderson recognized Shep, the jailer.

"Kickapopoulis, you take the cake!"

Kickapopoulis' massive face lighted

up. "Ho! We got cake, hah? Good!"

"You got the keys?"

"Keys? Sure. Hokydoke."

Henderson grabbed the keys as they were thrown across to him through the bars. As he let himself out of his cell, he tossed the keys back to Kickapopoulis and sprinted for the front door.

"Ho!" he heard the giant call. "Whoosa got the cake? Where you going, hah?"

"Trouble hunting!" Henderson flung back over his shoulder.

He found Shep's revolver in a desk drawer and slipped it into his holster. He left the jail, ran across the street to the sandwich stand. He jerked open the door of a powerful looking coupe, crowded in beside a startled young man.

"Out!" Henderson snapped tersely. "I'm commandeering this car!"

The young fellow opened his mouth to object, took one look at Henderson's blazing eyes, and closed it again without uttering a sound. He slid out. Henderson had the motor turning before the fellow hit the ground.

The two broad beams of the headlights carved a solid chunk from the blackness of the night. The motor, revving up nicely in the cool night air, flung its open-throated roar back into Henderson's ears. The sound was like soothing balm on the painful pang of fear that stung in his stomach. He was worried about Mary, afraid that he would be too late.

His frayed nerves sent his sharp eyes scanning the sides of the road—long before it was time, he knew. The throat of the old road would be bottled up with weeds. The fence would stretch across it in an unbroken line. He was depending partly on memory, partly on the instinct that won't let men forget paths of life once well travelled.

It was that instinct that found the place for him at last. He pulled the car from the highway, got out and ran along the barbed-wire fence until he found a post where the wires had been clipped, then stapled back on. Using a pair of pliers from the coupe's tool kit, he clipped them again, drove the car through the gap. He was aware of a car roaring up the highway behind him even as he opened his own throttle.

The ground was rocky and he knew there was little use of looking for tire marks here. The old road had been obliterated by the years, but ancient land marks kept jolting his memory, assuring him that he was on the right trail.

IT SEEMED ages before he came to Moon Hill River. He got out. With the aid of a flashlight from the coupe's kit he eagerly scanned the blue clay. His heart leaped as he found fresh tire marks.

A grin split his face. A deep, savage grin. He patted the gun in his holster, liked the weight of it against his hip.

He left the coupe. To drive farther would be foolhardy. Fording the river, he took up the trail on the other side. The road was better defined over here. The trees were so tall that there was very little underbrush, which probably explained how the old road had kept its markings through the years.

Henderson stumbled occasionally in the old ruts, daring to use the flash only in brief glimpses through shuttered fingers.

He came on the clearing so suddenly that it took his breath away. The old cabin reared its logs in a single story straight ahead of him. There were lights in the windows, and the outline of the bandit car showed against them. A car radio was playing soft music.

Henderson made his way across the

clearing, carefully picking up and putting down his feet. A distant humming told him where the river ran over the falls. Here the water flowed quietly, with only an occasional gurgle. The sound of raucous laughter and the click of chips told him that the bandits felt secure in their hideaway.

A treacherous twig snapped beneath his foot. He made the side of the cabin in three bounds and crouched there, his heart trying desperately to kick a hole in his ribs.

"What was that?" a startled voice cut through the open window.

He heard Killer Carmen's nasty laugh. "Monk, you got the jitters. Just some animal. Raise you ten."

The clink of chips bore out the Killer's bet.

"And ten more," Henderson heard Monk growl.

Henderson let the breath whistle softly through his teeth. His brow felt as though it had been sprayed with icy water. He mopped it.

The first thing he had to do was to locate Mary and be sure she was out of the line of fire. To get her out of the cabin first was out of the question. The old floorboards would creak like an ancient winch at every step.

He crept from window to window. Finally he located her lying helpless on an old rusty bed in one of the dark rooms. Enough of the lamplight filtered through the half open door to show him her taped wrists and ankles and the gag. Her eyes were wide and startled as she caught sight of him. He blew her a silent kiss and crept toward the lighted window.

Cautiously he peered around the edge. Too late he saw there were only two men in the room. Even as he started to whirl the bore of a gun bit into his back.

He cursed viciously through his teeth. That "Raise you ten" of Killer Carmen's had fooled him completely. He didn't even wait for the Killer's order to drop his gun, since it was as certain as taxes and death.

"Turn around, Copper!" The Killer's voice had the sound of water dripping on red hot steel.

Henderson started to turn, felt the stinging contact of the gun-barrel above his ear. It wasn't hard enough to knock him out—just hard enough to drop him to his hands and knees. He clutched the ground and got a handful of pebbles. His body screened the motion he made toward his mouth.

"So you can't stay put?" the Killer went on in his deadly voice. "I thought that wreck finished you. I'll take care of you myself this time! Get into the house!" His voice became a throaty snarl. "Go on, get moving, or I'll let you have it here!"

Henderson stumbled into the cabin, Carmen's gun barrel prodding heavily against his back. He seated himself in an old leather chair at Carmen's snarling command.

"Bring the dame, Monk," the Killer growled.

Henderson thought the name "Monk" very appropriate. The long, hairy arms of the man seemed almost to sweep the floor as the gangster waddled toward the bedroom door on short, bowed legs.

Henderson's face was like brown, hard rock. He didn't change expression as Monk dumped Mary into a chair. The oil lamp on the rickety table behind him sent its quiet light over his shoulder. It showed him the fresh, raw grief on the untaped part of Mary's face.

Her eyes above the gag smoldered with a strong hate for him. He wasn't surprised and he didn't blame her. The radio had undoubtedly told her about Smooty Schultz.

"By God, there'll be one less smart copper and one less mouthy dame in the world by morning!" The Killer's voice was in his usual throaty snarl, but his eyes had taken on an insane glitter. He licked his lips with a quick darting motion of his tongue.

The other bandit, whose nose was only a broken blob in the center of his face, licked his lips after Carmen, like a mimicking monkey. Monk growled with impatience. They all had their guns trained on Henderson.

THE music cut off on the car radio and an announcement came clearly through the open windows of the cabin. "We interrupt this program to bring you the latest bulletin on the Sunnydale Bank robbery. Mr. M. N. Jeeter, president of the bank, who was wounded in the robbery, just died in the Sunnydale Hospital. Before he expired he made a deathbed confession to police. He stated that he was short in his accounts at the bank and had arranged for Killer Carmen to rob the bank so that Jeeter could cover his losses by claiming more money had been stolen than Carmen actually took. The Killer double-crossed him and shot him, too. He also stated that Smooty Schultz was not in with the bank robbers, as police first suspected. Schultz died a hero's death trying to prevent the robbery."

The blood leaped and pounded in Henderson's head and sang a song of gladness in his ears. A grin covered his face suddenly and he felt like whooping with joy. Smooty Schultz hadn't let him down!

He watched the panorama of emotion pass through Mary's eyes. Wonder and remorse and love replaced the hate in rapid succession.

The Killer snarled and leaped to Mary's side. He grabbed her arm and twisted it cruelly. "How do you like that, Copper?" His eyes were small pinpoints of maniacal hatred.

Glistening beads of sweat formed on Henderson's forehead as he watched Mary's eyes fill and her throat swell against the gag. He restrained an impulse to dive at the leering killer; to take his chances against overwhelming odds. He sensed this would be what Carmen wanted.

He wondered if he had lost the prowess of his school days as he let go with the pebble in his mouth. He hadn't. It took the Killer squarely in the neck. Carmen slapped a hand to his neck and yelled, "Ouch!"

Both Monk's and Blobby Nose's eyes swivelled to the Killer. This gave Henderson the break he hoped for. He slammed all his weight onto his heels. The old leather chair crashed over backwards and he kept his body turning in a perfect somersault. His hard brogans caught the rickety table and sent it crashing into the far wall. The room was smashed into darkness for a moment and Henderson came to his feet clutching one of the table legs.

The oil from the lamp caught and the wall sprang into flames, showing Monk standing in front of him, gun hand tense. Flame danced from the automatic and Henderson heard the whisper of death go by his head even as he cracked Monk's skull with the table leg.

A slug nipped Henderson's shoulder, helped his spin toward Carmen. He flung the table leg at the Killer, followed it as the gang leader ducked, and felt his shoulder plow into Carmen's knees. They crashed to the floor.

Blobby Nose, standing by the door, was shooting wildly.

"Ho! Wotsa thees? Somebody looking for to get kill', hah?"

Henderson's heart leaped. Kickapopoulis! The big fellow had evidently followed him, probably got lost at the river, then been attracted by the light in the cabin.

The heat was bringing glistening beads of sweat to Henderson's face. He heard Blobby Nose bleat with terror as a hand like a giant bear's paw caught him alongside the head. There was a sickening crunch and Blobby Nose went sailing across the room to crack and fold up against the opposite wall.

Henderson saw Killer Carmen's eyes pop like grapes at the sight of the giant in the dancing flames. Carmen obviously couldn't believe the evidence of his eyes. He screamed in agonized fear and lined his automatic on Kickapopoulis.

Henderson climbed the Killer as though he were a fallen tree, one hand searching for the gun, the other a balled streak of knuckles. He missed in his grab for the gun and he heard the crack of the automatic even as his fist exploded against Carmen's jaw.

Kickapopoulis dropped.

A lump came into Henderson's throat and he cursed savagely as he kicked Killer Carmen in the head for insurance. He ran lightly to Kickapopoulis' side and dropped to a knee. The constricting bands of fear about his heart relaxed suddenly.

There wasn't a scratch on the big fellow.

Kickapopoulis opened one eye, evidently expecting to explore the Golden Gates. Then the other popped open.

"Ho!" he boomed. "So I'm not dead, no?"

The dammed up emotion in Henderson let go all at once. He laughed until the tears streamed down his cheeks. He caught up Mary in one strong arm and the bank loot in the other, and strode through the cabin door. Kickapopoulis carried out the three bandits as effortlessly as though they had been three pillows.

When Henderson removed Mary's gag, she was laughing as loud as he was. Then she sobered suddenly.

"Tom," she said earnestly. "I was wrong—dead wrong. From now on I cook for you and—and all your strange friends."

She looked toward the huge Kickapopoulis, who had perked up noticeably at the word "cook," and heaved a deep sigh.

"Even Kickapopoulis," she said resignedly.

Trooper Bill Lawson had never been shot at by a girl —and that was the starting point of a very busy vacation

A man in the shadows of the station crumpled and sagged to the floor

Trooper's Vacation

By L. K. Frank

AT SUNDOWN, State Police Private Bill Lawson, on vacation from the other end of the state, was tooling along toward Lake City and dodging the homeward-rushing traffic of suburban commuters. The city-bound lane of the road was nearly empty, but suddenly a yellow roadster snaked out of the outbound traffic and forced Bill to swerve his coupe violently into a fortuitous gas station driveway.

"The sun of a gun!" he cussed, "If I was working I'd chase the wheels off that Sunday driver." His abrupt maneuver had stalled his engine beside a gas pump, and he reckoned he might as well get gas, so he played a tattoo

93

on the horn button. His cop's eye saw a blue sedan parked at the curb, and his man's eye saw a burnished blonde mop sitting in the driver's seat, as he waited for the attendant. The blonde mop wouldn't give him a tumble, and since the attendant didn't come a-running either, Bill was about to tramp impatiently on the starter. As his foot reached for it, a faint 'Crack!' came from the station, and a window of the coupe shattered.

Bill was agile; he fell out of the door on his side of the car and came up with his Police .38 barking and spitting. A man in the shadows of the station crumpled and sagged to the concrete floor as a pistol flew out of his hand and clattered against the wall. The motor of the sedan at the curb roared, nearly drowning out another shot from inside the sedan. Bill felt a red hot poker slam along his skull, saw the slug's hole in his car door, and heard the fender bumping of the suddenly-snarled traffic in the road. He dimly saw a pudgy man holding a handkerchief to his face pelt out of the station to the sedan, and watched groggily as the big car screamed off toward the city, weaving recklessly through the traffic. Then, after a period of deep, black sleep, he sputtered up through a shower of water to open his eyes and exclaim, "Quit trying to drown me, you sap."

The station manager said, "Okay, pal; I can use the water to clean up the mess you made on the floor."

Bill looked down from the desk where he had been laid out, and saw the man he'd plugged. "Just a kid, eh? Well, I don't like to be shot at when I'm off duty. You better phone the cops. No, make it the sheriff since we're outside the city line."

While the man phoned, Bill swung himself to sit on the desk edge, and surveyed the view in a mirror. His brand new, grey suit had mopped up all the oil in the driveway, his shirt collar was ripped open, and his hair straggled over his smudged and bloodied face. The traffic rushed by as before; probably the shots had been taken for back-firing, and the few drivers who saw anything at all just supposed he was a drunk who had fallen out of his car in the driveway. People intent on getting home in a hurry don't stop to investigate anything less than an earthquake.

The manager turned back from his phoning and Bill remarked, "Pretty sight to go on a vacation, ain't I?"

The other grinned, but before he could reply a bulky man with an air of authority filled the doorway, and scowling at the apparition on the desk, demanded, "What's going on here, Webb? You know the rule against loafers in the stations."

Bill spoke up: "A little shooting practice, and who's a loafer?"

For the first time the newcomer's eyes fell on the corpse near a corner. "Hell's bells! Another one, Webb?"

"Yes, sir, Mr. Mason. This man here was waiting for gas, and plugged the kid when he started shooting. But Lumpy got away, Blondie driving, as usual. Fifty bucks this time."

A car rolled up to the curb behind a whining siren and the three men in the station looked out to see the sheriff and a couple of deputies tumble out in a tangle of riot guns, sidearms, and long clubs. A mongrel pup panting on the sidewalk seemed to be grinning at this inefficient display, and got a kick in the ribs for thus ridiculing the Law. Bill stiffened; he liked dogs, and the kick was uncalled for. But the dog, after a yelp and a jump, sat down and resumed his grin. Bill relaxed as the new arrivals piled into the station and Mason said wearily and without preliminaries:

"Too late again, Bartlett. As district station supervisor, I'm telling you that I'm going to close up every company station in the territory if you don't corral this Blondie and her gang."

The man who had kicked the dog answered, "Hell, I ain't got half enough deputies to protect every station in the county all the time. Who did this shooting, and who's the bum on the desk?"

"Maybe," Bill answered for himself, "I don't look very spruce just now, but 'bum' is the wrong name. I'm *mister* Lawson, to you."

The sheriff deliberately transferred his pistol to his left hand then flicked out his right and slapped Bill's face.

The next thing the sheriff knew he was on the floor, spitting out a tooth and looking at the muzzle of his own gun as it covered the room steadily.

"Sheriff, that tooth is for the pooch outside," Bill said conversationally. "It'd be a real pleasure to get another sometime, if we ever meet socially. Tell your boys to keep their artillery muzzled; this thing might go off and hurt somebody before I can get the feel of it."

The sheriff growled inarticulately at the deputies, and Bill went on, jerking a thumb toward the corpse of the bandit, *"He* might have been a bum, I dunno. But, this is me." He reached into a pocket and brought out an official-looking identification card, handing it to the sheriff.

"There y'are," he said, " 'Private William H. Lawson, Troop B, State Police. Age, Twenty-nine. Weight, Two hundred pounds. Height, Six feet. Eyes, Blue. Hair, Black.' "

The sheriff, looking from the card to Bill, snarled, "Why didn't you say so?"

"Why, sheriff, you never asked. You kind of jumped to conclusions, and landed wrong. I don't take that kind of pushing around when I'm on vacation." Bill broke the sheriff's gun, dumped the cartridges in his pocket, and tossed the gun on the floor.

WHEN the sheriff and his deputies left, Mason spoke up, carefully polite, "Mister Lawson, would you like to earn a nice piece of vacation money?"

Bill narrowed his eyes. "What's the lay?"

Mason answered, "This Blondie and her sidekick, Lumpy, have a gang of kids like the one you shot. Apparently Blondie picks up some boy, gets him on the needle, then when he's loaded and ripe, she and Lumpy take the punk out to stick up a station. You saw the technique; Blondie drives, Lumpy's the overseer, and the kid handles the gun. If the kid gets bumped, nobody cares. Blondie covers Lumpy from the car."

Bill interjected, "Where do I come in?"

"Right here, Mister Lawson: The stations in this corner of the state are losing too much money; fifty bucks here, seventy-five there. It's a rare week that Blondie doesn't clear four, five hundred. The Dealer's Association is offering a thousand dollars for Blondie and Lumpy, preferably dead. I will undertake that my company will kick in another thousand. Want to try it?"

"I should be a postman and take a walk on my day off, huh?" Bill said. "Nuts. But thanks just the same." He put his hand up to scratch his head, and winced as he touched the furrow in his scalp. "Hey! Wait a minute. So it was this Blondie who parted my hair? M-m-m. Well, that's something else. I guess I'll have to look into this, after all, because I never been shot at by a woman before, and I'd like to meet her, I would."

"Fine!" Mason answered. He handed Bill a card. "Call me if you need help. But remember, no Blondie, no pay." He left.

Bill stooped to examine the corpse that the sheriff had left for the morgue wagon. A nondescript, pimply-faced youth, such as decorate questionable poolrooms in any city. There was a hypo syringe in his pocket and some Remington .22 longs, but nothing else of interest. His gun lay under the desk out of sight, where it had fallen. Bill got down on his knees and gave a grunt of astonishment as he fished the gun out. It was a Winchester target pistol; a strange and clumsy weapon, with its long barrel, to be used in a holdup. He picked it up, noting as he examined it that the serial number had been filed at.

He turned to Webb. "Say, what's this? A target gun for stickups?"

Webb answered, "Yessir. I dunno how come, but I hear that mob always uses 'em. The sheriff's picked up two or three in the last month, around here. Every once in a while a station man, or somebody, plugs one of these kids, like you did today, and the gun gets turned in. You must have buffaloed the sheriff for fair, to make him forget it."

"Okay. I'll take it along." After he had brushed off his clothes and cleaned up as best he could in the washroom, Webb handed him his own gun from the desk drawer, where the station man had put it when he brought Bill

into the station. Bill slipped it into his shoulder holster and went out. He got the gas for which he had originally stopped, and started into town. A couple of blocks from the station he stopped again, took vials, a powerful lens, and his flashlight—it was now dark—from the shelf of the coupe, and succeeded in bringing out faintly the serial number of the gun. He memorized the number.

That done, he sat thinking a moment about the speed with which the sheriff had answered the alarm at the station. Presently he became aware of a pain in his innards. Diagnosing it as hunger, he locked the car and stepped across the street to a diner, which, from the tractor's outfits in the yard, was evidently a trucker's hangout. The diner was crowded but as Bill entered, two men left a couple of adjoining low counter stools, and he sat down on one. He had hardly ordered when an affectedly demure little brown-eyed, brown-haired trick came in and sat down next to him. She dropped her purse, and Bill, recognising the opening, bent to pick it up. Brown-Eyes smiled at him with a put-on friendliness.

"Thanks, Big Boy," she said. "Uh, I know most of the drivers, but I never saw you before. Who do you drive for?"

"Me? Oh, I drive for the state," Bill replied airily.

"Pooh. There's no state truck outside."

"Nope. I don't push a truck; I'm kind of inspector. But I'm off just now. Who do *you* drive for?"

Brown-Eyes didn't seem sure how to take his question, and conversation lagged while they both ate. When he was almost through with his meal the purse dropped again, and when he came up with it this time she had a little gun partly concealed in a fold of her jacket, ready for his inspection.

"Keep your hands in sight, brother, and let's get out of here," she said.

"For goodness' sake!" Bill exclaimed, in genuine surprise. He recovered quickly, however, and said, "Now, just a minute. If I keep my hands in sight I can't pay my check, and that wouldn't do, because I've never let a lady pay my fare yet. Here, let's do it this way." He handed the purse to her, and as she reached out to take it he dropped it on her gun hand, and followed the purse with a lightning dart of his own hand, seizing her wrist and deflecting the gun muzzle. "Leggo, or I'll snap your wrist like a toothpick," he murmured.

If the girl had any doubt that he would do as he threatened, the grip on her wrist was convincing. She released the gun, which he caught in his other hand and slipped invisibly into is coat pocket. If anyone had seen or heard the incident, it might have passed as a friendly scuffle, in the bustle and clatter of the place.

"Beat it, now, and pay your own check," Bill grinned. The girl glared at him, her eyes sparkling hate. He urged, laughing at her, "But don't go off in a pet; I could turn you in if I wanted to." She went in a pet, nevertheless.

IN HIS car again, Bill examined the gun he had taken from the girl: a pearl-handled .22 automatic, dainty and toylike, but capable of killing a guy at close range. "Two twenty-twos in two hours," he thought. "Aside from the fact that that's terrible alliteration, it's also too much coincidence. Blondie? Obviously not. This gal had no blonde mop like hers. A stooge for Blondie?

Maybe. And maybe just a dame looking for do-re-mi. But anyhow . . ." He went back to the diner washroom and with a strip of cord fastened the gun inside his trouser leg above his knee, smiling meanwhile. He was reminded of the cartridges from the sheriff's gun, and scooped them from his coat pocket. His eyes popped slightly as he exclaimed, "Good gracious!" Three of the shells were blanks. When he returned to the car, which he had left unlocked this time, the target pistol was missing from the shelf, so he reckoned he was being followed.

He drove on downtown, registered at the Lake Shore Hotel, and sent a night letter to the factory which had turned out the marksman's gun, asking that the serial number be traced in a hurry. He also called his lieutenant in the eastern end of the state and got formal permission to do a little private investigating while vacationing.

Then he called Mason: "I'd like to know, Mr. Mason, if your sheriff has ever plugged one of Blondie's gang himself, personally."

Mason answered, "Yeah. It's a funny thing. Sheriff Bartlett has just by coincidence happened along on two different occasions in the last six weeks while Blondie was pulling her stunt, and each time he knocked off one of these kid hopheads. But not soon enough to save the dough, either time."

"And he never pinked Lumpy or Blondie, huh?"

"No. He fired at Lumpy once, some months back, at our Bellevue road station, and missed. You understand, Lumpy stays in the background, and Blondie protects him. She knocked the sheriff's hat off at Bellevue, covering Lumpy's sprint to the car."

"Sounds kind of like a Shrinking

Violet-and-Annie Oakley act," Bill commented.

"Eh? Oh, yeh, sure. But are you getting anywhere?"

"As a matter of fact, I am," Bill answered, and hung up. "I certainly am," he said to himself, "Getting out to Bellevue road, tomorrow morning."

He requested at the desk that any telegrams be sent to his room the next morning, then went up to nurse the splitting headache that had finally caught up with him.

The bellhop's knock awoke him at ten a.m. The wire stated that the gun he had inquired about had been one of six dozen shipped a year previously to the Empire Target Club in Lake City. Bill dressed thoughtfully, not forgetting to replace the small automatic inside his trousers.

"Um-m," he muttered. "Gun clubs in this state are supposed to have permits, licenses, that sort of thing." But at the City-County Building, he could find no record of any such outfit. One more chance: the express office. His trooper's shield helped, here. A previously lazy clerk, at sight of the shield, was only too happy to look up the files, which showed that a case of guns had been delivered to "J. Coleman, Sec'y., Empire Target Club, c/o Joe's Cafe," on Hill street.

He decided to go out to the Bellevue road first; the cafe angle could wait. At the oil company's station on the Bellevue road he was lucky enough to find on duty the man who had been in the place at the time of the early holdup.

"What do you know about this stick-up?" Bill asked him, after having introduced himself.

"Nuthin' much; it happened too fast. This kid and Lumpy come in here, and the kid pulls a gun and I hand over the dough to Lumpy. Then th' sheriff comes along and mows down the kid and loosens one at Lumpy, who is on th' lam, and Blondie pots th' sheriff's lid, and that's all there was to it.

"The sheriff was pretty lucky?"

"Yeah. I guess so. But no luckier than Lumpy. Th' sheriff fired at him right in th' doorway—not more'n ten feet or so—and never touched him. Lumpy kept his handkerchief over his face, an' kept right on to th' car."

"That's what I want to know. And thank you kindly," Bill said.

"Skip it. I hope you get that gang, mister. I need this job, but th' job wont do me any good if one of these doped punks gets too jittery sometime with a .22."

BILL drove back into town and left his car at the hotel garage, then hailed a cab and asked to be taken to the twenty-two hundred block, Hill street. He got out at the corner and strolled down to Joe's Cafe.

"It should have been named 'Sloppy Joe's'," he thought, after he had entered and ordered a cup of coffee. "I got it," he grinned to himself, "they wanted the guns for target practice on the flies."

It was late afternoon by this time, and apparently only a counterman was holding the place down, a surly lout whom Bill reckoned either too dumb, or too smart, to know anything. Still, he could try.

"When's the boss in?" he began.

"Whaddya wanna know for?" the counterman came back.

"I want to talk to him about eggs."

"We got all the eggs we want."

"Yeh. All bad," Bill cracked. He slid off his stool and added, "I guess I'll take a look in back. Maybe the boss came in and forgot to tell you."

The other looked at him glumly but said nothing, so Bill began to saunter toward the door to the kitchen. He had almost reached it when the counterman's voice reached him first.

"Hey, mug, come back here!" it rasped.

Bill glanced quizzically at the counterman then took another step toward the door. He heard the scrape of a drawer being opened, and turned to see an automatic in the man's hand. He shrugged, and walked back to his coffee, remarking, "All right, if that's the way you feel. But it's bum hospitality."

"Listen, mug, I don't like your talk, or your acts, or your looks, or any part of you. Beat it!" the other grated.

"That's explicit enough. You win. Just a sec till I finish this coffee." Bill raised the heavy cup to his mouth and took a sip. With the darting suddenness of chain lightning he flipped the mug of scalding coffee at the counterman's gun hand and simultaneously whipped a left to the jaw. The coffee mug and the gun thudded to the floor together. The counterman, falling, slammed backward against the glass-doored shelving, which crashed, and fell apart, dumping a stack of breakfast food cartons and canned goods on his inert body.

Bill got his gun out and covered the kitchen door, but nothing happened. He leaned over the counter and surveyed the wreckage, wagging his head in self-reproof.

He vaulted over the counter and picked up the fallen gun, holstering his own. Just to be sure the lug would be safe for a while, Bill tied and gagged him. He closed and locked the front door. Fortunately the window was curtained so that passersby could not see behind the counter. Bill started

for the kitchen. Cautiously he pushed open the swinging door and found just a grimy, greasy restaurant kitchen. At one end of the room was another door which he thought must be the cellar door, until he saw the expensive lock on it. He put his shoulder against the door and heaved. Although he'd broken open many a door in his time, he discovered this one was reinforced and wouldn't budge.

Shooting the lock out might make too much noise, especially after that racket behind the counter. Looking at the door, he snapped his fingers; it was mounted on ordinary door butts, and they were on his side. Chuckling, he slid the pins out of the butts and with a thin slicing knife from the table, pried the door out of the frame.

The musty air of a long-vacant building crawled into his nostrils, and a rat squeaked in a corner of the darkened room. The windows were covered with iron shutters. The room was entirely empty, but in a corner was another door. This one was locked, too, but it gave to his weight. He felt a switch on the wall and turned it. The light revealed a flight of stairs, and Bill, still carrying the counterman's automatic and the kitchen knife, crept down into a basement apartment, well furnished and with signs that it had been occupied recently. Very recently; a faint blue haze of tobacco smoke showed around the lamps that he switched on.

Under a bed he found a case of .22 target pistols. He found also a suitcase which he pried open with the knife, and he was intently estimating the amount of morphine and opium in the bag when a voice in the doorway behind him barked, "Stand up, you—with your hands in the air!"

Bill jerked his head around. No dice; he was covered not by one, but by two automatics. The erstwhile counterman held one of them. "Leave the rod on the floor," the other hood growled.

"Well, if you say so, all right," Bill answered.

"Smart guy, huh? Reach!"

Bill reached.

One torpedo stayed in the doorway, alert. The counterman approached Bill, kicked the gun away, then viciously swung him around and brought the butt of his automatic crashing down.

HE SWAM up through a horrible red fog, thrusting aside clubs and swords swinging and darting at his head, with each thrust seeming almost to tear his arms from their sockets. When the fog faded he opened his eyes to blackness and found himself lying on a damp concrete floor, his hands tied behind his back and his ankles bound together. He had been trying unconsciously to wrench off the wrist ropes. Now he lay still and waited for his head to clear.

He wriggled a bit, and managed a grim little smile; he could feel the kitchen knife far up his right coat sleeve. He had slipped it in the sleeve, handle first, during the moment's palaver by the bed, and when he raised his hands the little knife had slid nearly to his armpit. The thugs had missed it when they took the gun from the holster on the left side. It took an hour of tortuous and agonizing wriggling and sawing to work the knife down his sleeve and another hour to cut through the cord at his wrists.

When the cord parted, he relaxed with a groan, bringing his hands up to his head. His scalp was matted with blood, and his hands were wet and sticky and burning from the cuts on his wrists, but he had managed to avoid the arteries. Soon he struggled up to a sitting position, and as he leaned forward to cut the ankle ropes he almost whooped with joy, for he felt the toy automatic still safely hidden between his thighs. Ah! A gun and two good fists! What more could a guy want? Well, a drink would help.

He crawled around the utter blackness of his prison. It seemed to be a basement storeroom. There was one door, locked, and too strong for a man in his weakened state. Continuing his tour, his hands found cases of canned goods, piles of lumber and trash, and, unbelievably, an opened case of whiskey. "This'll be on the house," he muttered, opening a bottle.

Footsteps thumped down a stairway, and a streak of light appeared under the door. A muffled voice said, "Why don't we bump him and get it over with, Lumpy?"

Bill stiffened as another voice snarled, "Listen, I told you to stop callin' me Lumpy. And don't call Blondie Blondie, either, if you know what's good for you. Anyhow, what's your rush? He'll never get outta here alive. We don't bump him because Blondie wants that pleasure for herself. She hates Nosey Neds on principle, an' owes this guy somethin' besides."

"Aw, Lum—uh, Joe, I wanted to bump him when we caught him but Walt said no. He sent me for you and went out to try to find Bl—her. I coulda heated this dick as easy as not," whined the first voice.

"Fer Gossakes!" Lumpy's voice barked, "Will you shut up! C'mon, let's get somethin' to drink, and have a look at him."

Like a cat, Bill was on his feet and behind the door, the little automatic in one hand, whiskey bottle in the other. A light flashed on in the room and he had a moment to accustom his eyes to it, while someone on the other side of the door fumbled with a key ring and struggled with the balky lock. The door swung open and two men entered the room. The first one was the counterman, again. His glance swept the room and he stuttered, "He's g-gone!" As he turned and saw Bill behind the door he reached for his hip pocket. He hardly got his automatic out when Bill loosed the bottle at him, kicked the door shut, and fired at Lumpy, all in the wink of an eye. The bottle took the gangster in the temple, his eyes glazed, and he followed his gun to the floor. Lumpy, staggering slowly backward across the room, struggled futilely to get his gun out of his shoulder holster. He bumped into the wall and collapsed.

Bill went to him, and pocketing the little .22, pulled the fellow's shirt open. "Yep," he muttered, as he found the tiny hole the slug had made, "Right in the ticker. Kind of delayed action, but what the hell."

The hood who had stopped the bottle suddenly came to life and leaped for Bill. It was the foolish move of a half-stunned man; he should have tried for his gun that Bill had carelessly left lying on the floor. Bill swung around and up from his crouch, catching the torpedo square on the jaw. Although it was just one punch, it was a lucky one, and it carried the authority of a true roundhouse swing. The man went down.

Bill blew on his knuckles. "You're a glutton for punishment, if I ever saw one," he told the inert form. "Three times I have to put you to sleep!" This time he trussed the fellow with a piece of wire from the packing cases, and stuffed a sugar sack in his mouth. Then he put the counterman's automatic in his own hip pocket, and

transferred Lumpy's revolver to his own shoulder holster.

STEPPING out of the storeroom, he heard footsteps overhead, and dived behind some curtains hanging across a closet entrance. The click of high heels punctuated the heavier noise of masculine footsteps. Blondie!

With the counterman's automatic in one hand and Lumpy's gun in the other, he got set for action—and almost fell over when the first person who entered the room was Sheriff Bartlett. Behind the sheriff followed the other hood who had covered Bill from the doorway, previously. Then came a woman—a young woman, pretty, but with a hard-boiled air. Bill stared at her. Brown eyes, platinum blonde hair. No, it didn't jell, though he was sure he had seen her before. The blonde mop—wait a minute: the girl put a hand to her head and swept off the platinum wig, and there she was; the meretriciously demure, little girl who had pulled the gunplay in the diner. He gulped down a gasp. Peeking from his retreat, he saw the torpedo eying the drapes intently, and decided it was time to act.

He stepped out and snapped, "Up, fast!" The torpedo moved quick, but Bill was quicker; his automatic barked and the heavy slug winged his man in the shoulder, spinning him around and dropping him in a heap.

Bill faced around instantly, and just in time. The sheriff's right hand had started dropping to his hip pocket, and Blondie apparently had designs toward a suspicious bulge under her left arm.

"Nix!" Bill exploded, and the hands reached upward again. "Well, well," he went on, "such company for a sheriff. You're all washed up, sheriff. Wait till the jury hears how you helped Blondie set those poor dumb kids up to be murdered in cold blood—like you kicked that pup!—and how your blank cartridges missed Lumpy."

He addressed the girl in turn: "Blondie, I'm obliged to you for that little gun. Your pal, Lumpy, ran up against it a few minutes ago. He's finished. It's too bad you only got the sheriff's hat, out on the Bellevue road; a mite better shooting, and he would have got no more cuts out of your stickups and dope peddling. And penny-pinching on target peashooters."

A faint scraping drew Bill's eye back to the wounded hood, who was trying to reach his fallen gun. Bill blasted at the gun, sending it flying in a dozen pieces. The distraction occupied but a tick of time, yet as Bill swung again to the other two, he heard the sheriff's gun roar twice even as he pulled the trigger of his own gun. With no time for a size-up, he had fired by instinct when a corner of his eye saw the sheriff's first shot drop Blondie in a screaming huddle.

He waited through an amazed eternity, wondering why Bartlett had shot the girl, and why he himself felt no pain from the sheriff's second shot. But the pain didn't come, and dazedly Bill realized he hadn't been hit. His own bullet had got the sheriff in the stomach before Bartlett could pull the trigger a third time.

The sheriff was done for, and Bill stooped over him to catch the man's dying words: ". . . damn witch . . . got me into this . . . finished her."

Bill slowly stood erect, breaking the sheriff's gun. Blanks and loaded shells alternated in the chambers. "Ha! I thought so," he said aloud. "So that's how he 'missed' Lumpy so often—and me, too, just now. Every other shot a blank! Lucky for me, but it must have been a bother for Bartlett to remember about."

A glance at the moaning Blondie told him that she had only a flesh wound in the arm. He ripped off a piece of the bed sheet and stepped over to bind up her arm. "Shush your caterwauling, Blondie," he said, "and let's hear what the sheriff got for his—uh, 'cooperation' with you and Lumpy."

"Too damn much!" the girl snarled bitterly. "And asking more all the time. I wish I'd got him, out at Bellevue. When I started in this racket, I thought he was a sap. But I found out *I* was the sap; he could turn us in any time, but who'd believe me if I tried to pin some of it on him? Ouch! Hey, be careful with that arm!"

Bill bound up the wound. "Shush! Don't carry on so high; you're supposed to be a tough moll. You spoiled a swell vacation but I sure learned about women from you!"

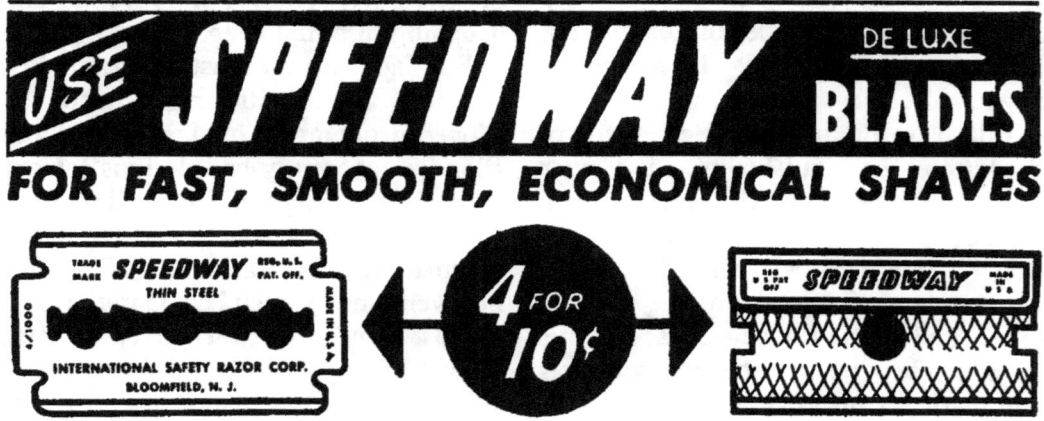

A Gal Named Sal

Rick Boston looked for the man with the wax-white face with only hope and revenge to go on

He hurled his shot up, aiming for the man's hat

By

C. S. Montanye

T HE wire was from his old lady. It had been sent to Headquarters and forwarded from there to his boarding house. Rick Boston read the telegram again:

ARRIVING TO-NIGHT. CALEDONIA EXPRESS. MOTHER.

His mouth twisted in a bitter, sardonic smile. He walked to the window, staring into the snow-blanketed street. Something as cold as the wind from the river bit into him.

He could never tell the old lady what had happened. How could he possibly explain that Deputy Commissioner McPhail had stripped him of his badge, thrown him off the force? Only that morning. Eight hours ago. Hauled in before the DC, broken and read out of the Department!

A fine greeting for a mother who thought the sun rose and set in her policeman son.

Rick sat down on the edge of the bed. His nervous fingers twisted the yellow telegram.

Finally he stuffed it in his pocket, got up and put on overcoat and hat.

In the lower hall he dropped a nickel in the telephone and called the Union Station.

"What time's the Caledonia due?"

"She'll be late to-night. Hour or more. Lot of snow up the line. Might be after one o'clock. Call back in a couple of hours."

"Okay, thanks."

He hung up and went out. The thermometer had dropped. The wind was like a knife, but Rick didn't mind that. He had been inwardly frozen all day. Mechanically he headed toward the cluster of lights over the amusement area of the city.

He walked fast, thinking of the man with the wax-white face and the burning, deep-set eyes. If he could only find that lug again! If he could only bump into him somewhere! If he could only get a hand on him, jam him into a corner and make him talk!

The man with the wax-white face was the cause of it all. He had come up to Rick last Wednesday night, Rick was almost ready to go off beat. He had ten minutes more. He was on duty, patrolling the street on which 'Bug' Rossi, the wop political leader, lived.

Rossi had propositioned McPhail. The politician had gotten warning letters. He was afraid, deadly afraid, some of his erstwhile · friends were ready to hand him a harp and a bunch of lilies.

Rick had been assigned to the neighborhood. Four nights without so much as a taxi's backfire. Four nights of wind and cold and bright, twinkling stars. Then Wednesday, the guy with the dead, colorless pan.

He had come up out of nowhere. He had asked Rick what time it was and, when Rick unbuttoned his blue service coat to fumble for his watch, the man had tapped him on the side of the head. Just like that, as easy.

There had been general hell to pay. It seemed Mrs. Rossi had telephoned for the cops. Bug had been kidnapped, hijacked right out of his cosy living room by three or four toughies who had forced their way in. Snatched and whisked away in a big black sedan.

They found Rick in the areaway, stinking of whisky and with a bruise above his left ear. Supposedly, he had gotten that when, in his drunken stupor, he had slipped on the ice and cracked his conk on the top stone step. That was the DC's version and nothing could shake it.

Rick's set lips twisted again as he hurried on. A mug with a wax-white face. His old lady due on the Caledonia, and he, in exile, broken, booted out.

So far as he knew there hadn't been a smell of Bug Rossi. The politician had disappeared into thin air. Rick buried his chin in his coat, turning into Congress Boulevard.

THE neon signs of theaters, movie houses and night spots made a pageant of light. Rick went on as far as the Oasis. He slowed as he approached the ornate facade. Outside, in metal frames, photos of the little lovelies appearing in the floor show smiled at him. Rick's gaze darted to the one in the middle.

Her name was Sal Niven. She was blond, beautiful. Had she actually been there under the marquee, instead of just a picture, she would have frozen to death. She didn't wear enough to keep a department store dummy warm in a steam heated window.

"Hello, copper. Going in?"

The door man loomed up beside

Rick. He was a big guy in a costume that looked like a rear-admiral's uniform. An ex-con trying to make a come-back. Funny, Rossi had gotten him the job. But that was all right, too. The Bug owned a chunk of the nightery. A lot of his pals worked around in places Rossi backed.

"Yeah, might be an idea," Rick answered.

Reluctantly he tore his gaze from the piquant face of the gal named Sal and went through the revolving door. He checked his flogger and skimmer with the little brunette at the coat room counter and walked in to the foyer.

He wondered just why he had come. So many other nights, when he was through work, he had dropped around to watch Sal hoof and warble. But to-night was different. To-night he wasn't the Rick Boston of last week.

To-night he was a cop who had been let out—found drunk on duty, canned.

He sat down at a table to the left of the doors. The first floor show was underway. The pretties were swinging shapely daisy-stems in a rhythmic line and cooing about a Hawaiian moon.

Rick ordered a bottle of ginger ale and lighted a cigaret. His gaze went around the customers. Same crowd as usual. Cheap guys with their cheap gals. The riffraff of the city. Here and there a spender, maybe one of Rossi's henchmen. As political boss of the South End, Bug had been more than generous in passing out his favors.

Suddenly Rick straightened up. The gal named Sal had come on for her specialty. The calcium moons melted into an amber flood. In its glow Sal was like some golden dryad that had crept out from an enchanted glen.

Her voice held husky, sweet tones which haunted Rick Boston with poignant appeal. He wondered if he had gone and gotten himself in love with Sal.

The floor show ended. Rick finished his ginger ale. He paid the check and threaded a way through the tables to a rear door which opened into a passage near the kitchen and stairs.

Rick went up the steps. On the landing were the dressing rooms. The girls were hurrying into them. Rick went over to the second door to the left and knocked.

Sal's blue eyes looked out at him from the partly opened door. "Hello, Rick. I thought I saw you downstairs a while ago. Come in, I'm decent."

He rested on a trunk and his eyes drank her in thirstily. A faced robe pulled tight, outlined her slender figure. The murky light made her yellow hair glimmer with a golden motif. Her eyes were like dusky stars in the pale heaven of her oval face.

"It happened this morning," Rick began slowly. "McPhail took my badge I'm out."

"Oh, Rick!" Her voice held all the quick sympathy that was part of her nature. She wheeled around. Her hand tightened on his arm. "I'm sorry, that's tough."

"But I'm not through. They're not going to frame me. Sometime I'll be back, be around again."

"How?"

"When I find a certain party." Rick drew a breath. No use boring her with the dull, heavy ache in his heart. He tried to smile. "My old lady's coming in tonight. I've got a room at the boarding house for her. After I get her at the depot, how about a date?"

The blue eyes grew pensive. They looked over Rick musingly. She appeared to be thinking. Finally she nodded and took a key out of the leather bag on the vanity.

"I don't know why I do this. Maybe because I'm sorry for you. Here, this will let you in the flat." She handed him a saw-toothed key. "Better wait up there. I'll be in after the last show."

"You don't want me back here?"

"No, not tonight."

His gaze held hers. "Why?"

"Don't ask so many questions. Duck now. I'm going to relax—"

RICK went down to Congress Boulevard. He phoned the Union Station from a nearby drugstore booth. "The Caledonia stalled at Granby Falls," he was told. "It's snowing hard up there, switches are frozen. We don't know when she'll be in, probably not before morning. If you'll call again in a couple of hours—"

Rick hung up and went out on the street. There were a couple of cabs parked below the Oasis. He was about to grab one when a man, coming out of the night club, beat him to it.

Something in Rick flared up like a kerosene-soaked rag at the touch of a match. The man leaned over to speak to the driver. The neon lights threw his face into sharp silhouette. Rick, transfixed, saw again a wax-white complexion, burning, deep-set eyes.

His man!

The first cab was off like a shot. Rick flung open the door of the second and jumped in.

"Follow that ark!" he ordered. "Tail him and be smart about it!"

Manny Fink, the driver, looked over his shoulder. "Yeah, who says—" He broke off. "Oh, Chief Boston. I didn't recognize you in your regular clothes."

"Don't let him get away!"

The first cab slid into the darkness beyond the amusement district. It scuttled west, then south. It went past the freight yards. Presently it was in Rossi's old political stronghold, the Italian district on the South End.

The cab stopped and the man got out. He wore a long, belted overcoat. Its collar was turned up and the brim of his felt hat snapped down. He went into a two-story building. There was a candy and cigar store on the street level. Manny Fink curbed discreetly some distance behind the first taxi and Rick got out.

He went in the candy store and looked at the magazine rack. The proprietor, a fat Italian, sat on a stool behind the cigar counter. Rick could feel his eyes boring into him. He bought a package of cigarettes and said:

"Any news about Rossi?"

"No, no news. The boss—he's gone. He won't never come back now. They got him."

"Who got him?"

The other yawned and shrugged his fat shoulders. "Some of those Chicago people. Mr. Rossi, he was doing too good here. You can't do good no-where. When you do, they muscle in. They don't want just a little bit. They want it all."

" 'Chicago people'?" Rick Boston cued.

"Sam Keller, his people."

The man with the wax-white face came out of the building. Rick saw him stride across the pavement, get back in the taxi. It snarled off, gears clashing. Rick was out and after him like a flash. But this time he wasn't so lucky. A slow, night freight had dropped the gates at the Grand Avenue crossing over which the first cab had hurried.

Cursing, Rick piled out. The dismal hoot of the freight's locomotive sounded. It came into view and the last thing Rick saw, before the train blocked his vision, was the red tail light of the fast disappearing taxi.

Rick sank back on the worn uphol-stery. A sense of frustration gripped him. For a few minutes his mind had soared. He had been sure he was play-ing in luck. He had found the white-faced man, who had framed him. He almost had his hands on that guy— almost had him ready to twist out in-formation that would explain a ques-tion that had numbed him since that Wednesday night.

Why had he been rigged and put in line for immediate dismissal? Why hadn't they knocked him off and called it a night?

"Where to, Chief?"

Rick raised his heavy gaze. The gates were up and Manny Fink was waiting for a destination.

"The Lester Apartments. Know where they are?"

THE cab rolled on. Rick's thoughts went to Sal Niven. She hadn't wanted him to come back to the Oasis for her. Why? He brooded, watching the streets melt past.

For a long time he had been buzz-ing around Sal. He couldn't help it. She had something—charm, personality and looks. But she was a funny kid. Mys-terious in a way. He had never been able to pump her, to find out anything about her personal life. Sal was friendly enough—sweet—but she dwelt behind a wall of reserve.

Rick's nails dug into the palms of his gloved hands. What would Sal want with a broken cop?

He rubbed breath fog from the glass beside him. He looked out the window. They were back on the west side and it had begun to snow. A fine, desultory fall already beginning to stick.

"Here we are, skipper."

The brakes caught, the front wheels skidded and the taxi thudded into the curb before the Lester Apartments.

Rick paid and tipped Manny Fink. He told him not to wait and went into the vestibule. He dug up the key Sal had given him. On the second floor he fitted it into the lock of a door that faced the stairs. He pushed the door open into warm, cloying darkness. He breathed in the unmistakable perfume that always clung to the girl as his fingers searched the wall for the switch.

Hanging coat and hat in the foyer closet, Rick went on to the living room beyond. He lit a lamp on a table at the end of a mohair divan and sat down.

What the proprietor of the cigar store had said came back to mingle with his heavy, depressing thoughts. The South End compatriots of Rossi knew more about his disappearance than the police.

And Sam Keller. Rick knew about that bird. One of Chicago's ace muscle-inners.

It looked as if Keller was getting ready to move in, take over and settle down in Rossi's domain.

The ring of the telephone broke in on Rick.

HE GOT up, unhooked the receiver. A girl's voice drifted across the wire:

"Is Sal Niven there yet?"

"No, she's at the Oasis."

"Who's this?"

"A friend of hers."

"Yes, but *who?*"

Rick caught the anxious, inflected note in the girl's voice.

"What difference does it make?"

"A whole lot! You—" She stopped, broke off and then added rapidly: "Are you Mr. Boston.

"That's right. You—"

"Listen. Listen carefully! I'm

Stella. I used to work with Sal at the Vendome. I was over at Gleason's Tavern tonight, a half hour ago. There were a couple of mugs there—in the compartment back of me. They were talking about Sal. They said she knew something! It didn't sound good to me—"

Rick's fingers tightened around the rubber receiver. "Take it easy. Don't talk so fast. Who were they? What else did they say?"

"I don't know who they were. I heard one of them tell the other that later on they were going to fix her so she couldn't—"

The connection suddenly broke. The wires hummed and buzzed in Rick's ear.

"Numbah, paleese."

Rick dropped the receiver back on its metal arm. In the foyer he shouldered on his coat, jammed on his hat. He half turned to switch off the overhead light when he saw something he hadn't noticed when he came in.

He clicked electricity on in a milk-white globe. He stood on the threshold of the kitchenette, momentarily dazzled by the glint of porcelain, enamel and chromium. His gaze darted to that portion of the black-and-white squared linoleum between the kitchen table and the sink.

The contorted figure of a man lay there. His face was against the floor. One arm was under him, the other outstretched, stubby, rigid fingers wide and talon-like!

Rick's heart pounded. A hot wave of fear made his stomach churn. He bent over the man. A touch was enough to tell Rick he had been dead for some time. When he turned the body over he saw the neat hole drilled into his forehead, close to his right eye.

An expensively tailored tweed suit, custom-made, twenty-two-bucks-a-pair shoes—a gay striped tie and a diamond ring glinting on one of the taut fingers.

Mrs. Rossi wouldn't have to worry any more about her politician husband.

The Bug had checked out!

In the living room Rick impatiently jiggled the hook for Central. He gave her a familiar number—waited, breathing in the perfume and the scent of the room.

"Headquarters? . . . McPhail gone? . . . Yeah, Inspector Dwight. . . . Hurry it." And then, after what seemed an interminable pause. "This is Boston speaking. I've found Bug Rossi! Dead! Dumped in a flat at the Lester Apartments! Two-C! The second floor—"

He left the lights and ran down the stairs. It was snowing harder. Wet flakes melted against his hot face.

Three streets further on Rick found a taxi. Its chains clanked against the wet pavement. Windshield wipers tried desperately to combat the burden of the snow.

"The Oasis! Drive like hell!"

THE neons still crawled colorfully across the front of the night spot. Rick jumped out. He shoved a bill into the driver's hand. He hurried from the foyer to the passage that led to the dressing rooms. He slowed, hearing the distant beat of the orchestra, the lilt of song.

Odd relief spread through him. He unbuttoned his coat. Perspiration trickled down under the band of his hat, but his hands were icy cold.

He went on to the dressing rooms. A tall boy who did a specialty dance number was propped up against one wall, sucking on a cigarette. Rick pushed open the door to Sal's room. He went in, shut it after him, threw off his coat and drew a sleeve across his damp face.

Two, five or fifteen minutes passed before she came in.

"Rick! I thought you were at the flat."

He shoved the door shut and gripped her bare arm. He pulled her around so she faced him. She wore the scanty costume of the show's finale. She winced away, but he wasn't looking at her gleaming skin. His strained worried eyes bored into hers.

"I just left the apartment! *You knew Rossi!*"

He could feel as well as see the spasm of startled surprise quivering through her body and widening her blue eyes. Her expression changed instantly.

"Rick! I—"

"What do you know about him? Why should he be up there in your apartment—"

"My—apartment!"

"Murdered! Come on, tell me! What are you hiding? I called Inspector Dwight. They'll have a squad around there any minute. They'll come down here to get you!"

"Rossi—dead!"

She collapsed, drawing her limp arm out of his grasp and sinking down in a chair before the dresser. Rick watched her. He was shaking inwardly, trembling for her as much as from the excitement possessing him.

Sal's hand groped toward her faded robe. She draped it around her. In the glass her eyes were blank, staring.

"Talk!"

She lifted her head. "I didn't know— they killed Bug. They were holding him downtown. It was Sam—Sam planning to take over! Six months ago he got the idea. The olive oil and spaghetti racket. The policy bank. Rossi's labor grift—all that stuff."

"What else?"

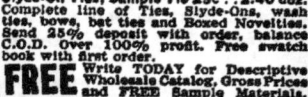
"I tried to head him off. I did everything I could."

"Keller? You—"

She nodded haggardly. "Yes, Sam. I'm his wife!"

Rick hung over her, stiff and bewildered. Sam Keller's wife! This gal he was nuts about—married to that sharpshooter! It was as if he had been kicked in the face. He could hardly breathe. He peered at her uncertainly.

"Sal!" His voice was husky and unnatural. "Why didn't you tell—"

"As if I were proud of it!" A whip of contempt lashed her tone. "I haven't lived with him for more than a year! I came here from Chi to get away! He followed me! I've been afraid—lately. Ever since he knew you were interested! I got this—"

She pulled open a drawer in the dresser. Rick saw the snub-nosed automatic lying there among cosmetic jars. Something like flame burned in his mind.

"Keller knew—I'd fallen for you—" He seized her arm again, jerking her forward. "Then—Keller—"

"Framed you! He's always been like that—insanely jealous! He thought I wouldn't care for you once you were broken—kicked out! He could have knocked you off, but you wouldn't have suffered then! He—"

"Come on!" Rick pulled her to her feet. "We've got to get out of here—fast! Stella phoned. She heard a couple of guys talking! About 'fixing' you! That means Keller and—"

THE dressing room door opened. A man with a wax-white face and deep-set burning eyes crossed the threshold. The collar of his belted overcoat was turned up, his felt hat pulled low over his face as if to shade his sultry eyes.

A younger, taller, powerfully built man followed him in. Rick heard Sal's throat-strangled exclamation. The thin, twisted lips of the Chicago killer cracked in a grimace. He said to the man with him:

"Let's have your biscuit, Bob—"

A gun changed hands. Rick, held supine, acted abruptly when life and reason flashed like lightning in on his stunned brain.

A thrust of his arm sent Sal to the floor. The reverberation of Keller's first shot filled the room with pounding echoes. The slug whistled past Rick's head and chunked into the plaster wall.

He had Sal's snub-nosed automatic out of the drawer in the next breath. It was off safety and ready for use. He hadn't practiced long hours in the range at Headquarters for the fun of it. He aimed and squeezed the trigger without being conscious of either act.

He felt his hand shake from the explosion of the weapon in it. He hurled his shot up, angling for Keller's hat. He could almost see the spray and splash of the lead as it hurtled into the bony structure between the man's eyes.

Keller pitched forward. The gun dropped from his hand. The man who had come in with him had it almost at the same minute it struck the floor. He fired from a crouching position, fast as he could level out.

Slugs tore through Rick's coat. The hat that he had neglected to remove whisked away. He heard the ping of the vanity's mirror as it splintered in a crystalline shower. A red haze, like gauze, came before his eyes. Outside he could hear the drum of feet, the shriek of voices, the scream of a police whistle. He fired once—twice—three times, willing the shots into the target of the crouching figure across the room.

The smell of burned power was acrid

in his nose and throat. The automatic was hot in his hand. He waited, eardrums throbbing with the pulsing echoes.

They died away presently. Only the riot outside sounded. The man who had come in with Sam Keller had squirmed over on his back. His convulsive twitching ended.

Rick tossed the warm rod back into the drawer. He sucked air, steadying himself against the chair out of which he had hurled Sal. He didn't know if he'd been punctured. He was only conscious of the girl's closed eyes and white face. She was in a huddle, half under the vanity.

Rick picked her up. He had no idea she was so light, such a meager armful. He carried her to the door, through it and out into the passage where frightened faces were a fleshy smear before his narrowed eyes.

"Get water! She's fainted!"

Someone guided him across the corridor and into a room where there was a couch.

After a long minute the lids of her blue eyes opened. She looked up at him. She smiled a little, confidently, happily, with a mouth still heavy with carmine.

"Rick!"

He bent over her. He laughed softly. He smoothed her cheek with the back of his hand and gave her the glass of water someone had brought.

"Drink this. And don't talk. Just relax. I—I'll be back in a minute—"

Her fingers caught and twined with his. "Where are you going—"

He got up. He looked down at her and there was a world of meaning in his gaze. Rick laughed again.

"Out to telephone. I've got to find out about a train that's overdue. We've got to meet it when it comes in. Our—our old lady's on it!"